Second Chance Summer

Written and published by Kait Nolan

Copyright 2017 Kait Nolan

Cover design by Najla Qamber

AUTHOR'S NOTE: The following is a work of fiction. All people, places, and events are purely products of the author's imagination. Any resemblance to actual people, places, or events is entirely coincidental.

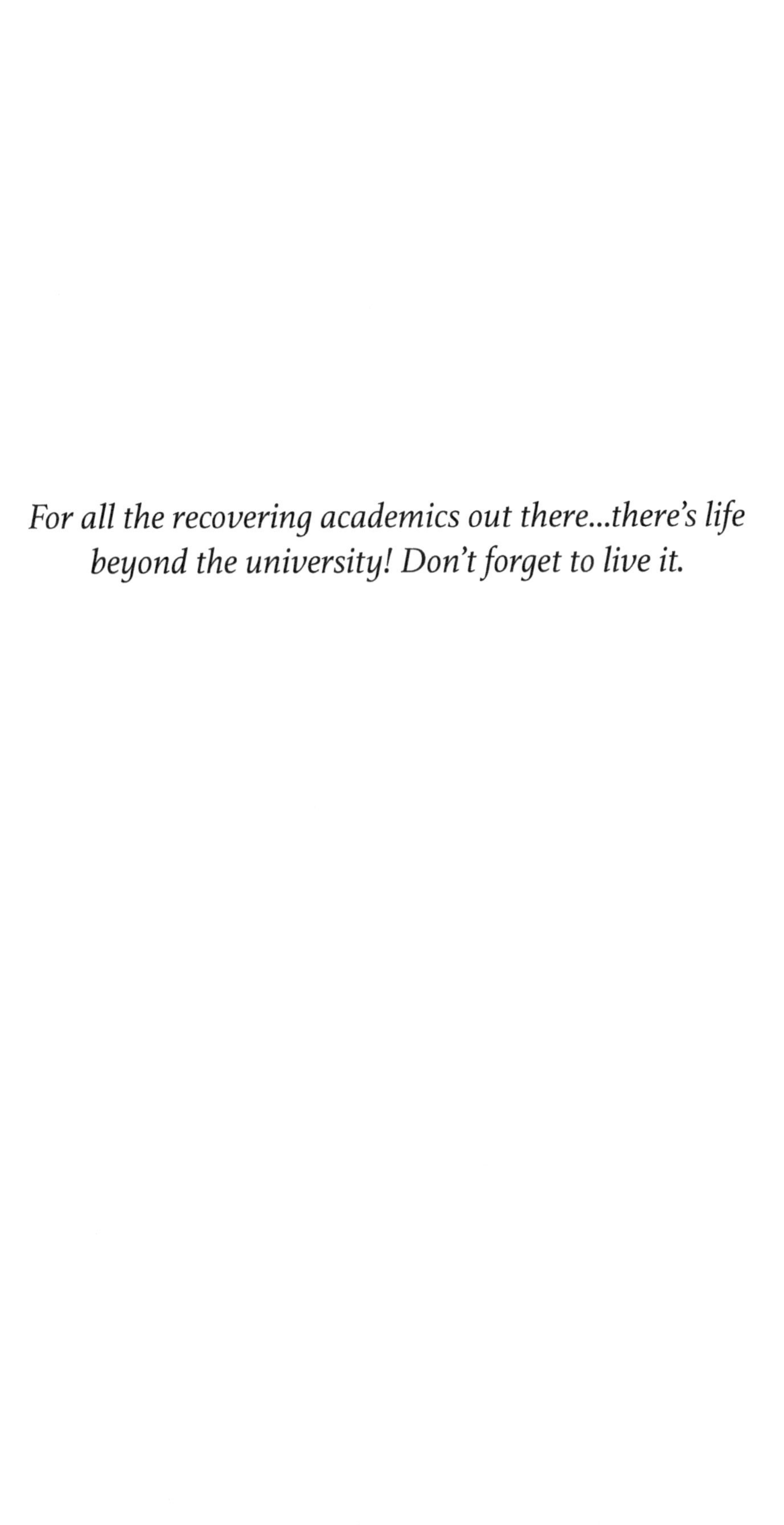

For all the recovering academics out there...there's life beyond the university! Don't forget to live it.

Do you need more small town sass and spark? Sign up for <u>my newsletter</u> to hear about new releases, book deals, and exclusive content!

Want to get social? Join me in <u>Kait's Cantina</u>!

A LETTER TO READERS

Dear Reader,

This book also contains swearing and pre-marital sex between the lead couple, as those things are part of the realistic lives of characters of this generation, and of many of my readers.

If any of these things are not your cup of tea, please consider that you may not be the right audience for this book. There are scores of other books out there that are written with you in mind. In fact, I've got a list of some of my favorite authors who write on the sweeter side on my website at https://kaitnolan.com/on-the-sweeter-side/

If you choose to stick with me, I hope you enjoy!

Happy reading!
Kait

1

"I'VE NEVER SEEN ANYBODY so excited to ride a bus before."

Audrey Graham gave a little bounce on the vinyl-covered bench seat, strangely delighted with the squeak of springs. "I've never been on one. I mean, not a school bus. Just the public transit kind."

Beside her, Samantha Ferguson, her partner in this adventure, chuckled and grabbed hold of the seat in front of them for balance as the bus lurched through a pothole. "Whatever floats your boat, sugar."

"If you're looking for an authentic school bus ride, I can always start a spitball fight." This came from the guy who'd twisted around from the next seat up. The mop of sandy hair and smattering of freckles across his cheeks made him look several years younger than he probably was. He stuck out a hand. "Charlie."

Was this what camp was like? All first names all the time? It was so different from the formality and pretentiousness of academia.

"Audrey. And this is Sam." They all shook hands.

"Where are you from?" Charlie asked.

"Little bitty town in northeast Tennessee called Eden's Ridge," Sam replied. "Though most recently Chattanooga. I teach at a small, private college there. So does Audrey."

For now. "I'm originally from Kansas City, though."

"Long Island. I work in Manhattan these days."

"Yeah? What do you do?" Audrey asked, unable to imagine this golden retriever of a man amid the stiff suits and stuffed shirts.

"I'm an assistant editor at Macmillan."

Sam brightened. "Yeah? What genre?"

"Don't laugh. Romance."

"Now you've done it," Audrey warned. "The book monster has awoken. Sam's an English Lit professor and romance aficionado."

"Really? I'd have thought you'd turn your nose up at romance."

"No way. I love it. I even teach a class on the development of the genre and its relation to feminist theory."

Audrey hid a smile as the two launched into an animated discussion of favorite authors. She had no idea if there were any prospective sparks there, but at least Sam had found a kindred spirit.

"Are you two returning campers to Camp Firefly Falls?" Charlie's question pulled her attention back to the conversation.

"First timers," Sam told him. "Audrey here is a summer camp virgin."

Audrey felt her cheeks heat with a blush and had no idea why. It wasn't like she was *that* kind of virgin.

Not exactly far off... her brain reminded her.

Shut up.

"No shit? Well, the Retro Session is definitely the way to go to get the experience," Charlie said. "I came here every summer, when I was a kid. Got super pumped when I found out it'd been turned into a camp for grown-ups."

"Me too I'm tackling some entries on my bucket list lately, and when I heard about Camp Firefly Falls, it seemed like an opportunity to knock a few out in one fell swoop." Which was the most understated way Audrey could possibly explain her reasons for being here. But spilling her guts to a complete stranger on the camp bus as they drove up from New York was not one of those bucket list items.

"So you've never been to camp, and you went to camp somewhere else?" Charlie asked, looking from Audrey to Sam.

"Hale River Camp and Farm, in North Alabama," Sam replied.

"That's a long way from the Berkshires. How'd you hear about Camp Firefly Falls?"

The flash of phantom pain in her legs kept Audrey from answering immediately. Riding the wave, she forced a smile. "Oh, someone I met once mentioned coming here as a kid. I guess the name stuck in my head."

"I'm just along for the ride and to get my nostalgia on," Sam put in. "I *loved* camp. Went every year, from the time I was seven—camper through counselor."

She and Charlie fell back into easy conversation, and Audrey let them, focusing instead on breathing through the ache. The novelty of the bus ride was wearing thin. She'd been sitting too long and her legs were beginning to cramp up. A walk would be in order as soon as they got their stuff dumped at the cabin. Maybe a stroll along Lake Waawaatesi. It had looked so picturesque in the promo photos online.

From the back of the bus, someone began to sing "She'll Be Comin' Round The Mountain" as they turned onto the long, winding road that would, according to the map Audrey had studied, lead up to Camp Firefly Falls. They were nearly there. Then she'd have two, long, glorious weeks with no cell phone, no email, no reminders of the career decisions she still needed to make. Two weeks to relax. Two weeks to take life by the horns and really live it. Which meant pushing herself out of her comfort zone. She'd become an expert at pushing herself the last two years. More than she ought to, according to her parents, but what did they know? If she'd listened to them, she wouldn't have anything resembling a life anymore.

Well, okay, that wasn't entirely fair. They meant well. They'd always meant well. But it was her life, and she was finally going to live it. Going to camp was just the latest in a long line of small rebellions. Who knew that she, of all people, would develop a taste for defiance at the ripe old age of twenty-seven? But was it enough to change her life over? That was part of what she was here to figure out. Maybe, by the end of session, she'd finally know what she wanted.

Abruptly, the lush green trees opened up and the bus turned beneath an arched sign that read *Camp Firefly Falls*.

"We're here!" Audrey couldn't keep the excitement from her voice.

A cheer swept the bus as they pulled into a gravel parking lot, where a blonde woman with a boathouse stood behind a folding card table, surrounded by a handful of staff members in Camp Firefly Falls t-shirts. Audrey was on her feet the moment they rolled to a stop. Her legs protested the rapid movement, and she had to grab Charlie's seat to catch her balance.

Sam slipped an arm around Audrey's waist to steady her. "Okay?"

"Just stiff. Let's get out."

They edged into the aisle and filed off the bus with the other campers. A couple of other staff members circled around to the back and began offloading luggage as Audrey, Sam, and the others got in a loose line at the table to register and pick up their cabin assignments.

"Hi!" The blonde offered up a wide smile. "I'm Heather Tully. My husband and I own the camp. Welcome!"

"We're so excited to be here. I'm Audrey Graham, and this is Samantha Ferguson."

"Excellent. You're in Cabin 7."

"Lucky number," Sam pronounced.

If this were one of the camp movies Audrey had binge watched before coming, some guy would make a crude joke about getting lucky in Cabin 7. Apparently, the Camp Firefly Falls alums were a little more discreet. Or maybe real life was less salacious than the movies.

"Now, if you'll just turn in your cell phones. We'll keep them locked up at the lodge, so no worries something might happen to them." Heather held out zip top bags with their names scrawled out in marker.

"No cell phones?" Sam asked, digging in her purse.

"It's a new rule we're trying out for the Retro Session. Cell phones weren't a thing back when we were kids at camp, and we're trying to get back to that feel as much as we can."

"Sign me up. I can't remember the last time I went a day without hearing a phone ring." Sam slipped her phone into the bag.

Audrey sent one last text off to her mom. **Arrived at camp safely. No phones allowed. I'll talk to you in two weeks.** Then she powered down and slid her phone into the other bag. Two whole weeks where her parents couldn't pressure her about Berkeley. That sounded like heaven.

Heather pulled out a map for each of them and circled Cabin 7. "If you head just up that trail and take the left fork, past the dining hall, you'll find your cabin ready and waiting. Dinner's going to be served at six, and we're having a little opening night mixer at the boathouse starting at seven-thirty. Come ready to dance!"

Audrey took her map. "We'll be there with bells on."

AT THE SIGHT of the bus turning onto the final road to Camp Firefly Falls, Hudson Lowell grimaced. The last thing he wanted was to get caught up in the crazy of drop off day with all the other campers. Was it even called drop off day now that they were all adults? Didn't matter. Either way, there'd be enough excitement and good cheer that he'd be liable to deck somebody. Better to kill a little time and circle back. There'd be no avoiding the walk down memory lane the next two weeks, but he could ease into it rather than leaping feet first. So, he drove on past the turn and kept heading north, wondering if Boone's was still in business.

Part gas station, part general store, part diner, Boone's had always been an official stop before his parents dropped him off to camp as a kid. Located halfway between camp and Briarsted, the nearest town, Boone's was the last bastion of civilization before two weeks of unfettered, summertime awesome. Ten minutes later, he pulled his Jeep into the lot. The whole complex was smaller than he'd remembered, but the scent of freshly brewed coffee was the same. It drew him back into the diner, where he settled into a booth and grabbed the laminated menu from between the napkin holder and the ketchup. He looked at the options without much interest.

A gum-chewing waitress appeared at the table, a pot of coffee in her hand. "What can I getcha, hon?"

"Just coffee. And a slice of pie." Pie was always a good idea.

She turned over the cup at his elbow and filled it near to the brim. "Apple or peach?"

"Peach. With ice cream."

"Comin' right up."

As she disappeared, Hudson slipped his phone out. Might as well make this last call before he got on up the mountain. Reception would probably be spotty.

"Hudson!"

"Hey Mom."

"Are you there yet? Is it fabulous? I'm so curious what all they've done to change the place since you were a boy."

He gritted his teeth against her cheer. "I haven't quite made it to camp yet. I stopped in at Boone's."

She laughed. "Of course. Couldn't go to camp for two weeks without your Twizzlers."

Had he even had a Twizzler in the past decade?

The waitress returned with his pie a la mode, and Hudson nodded his thanks.

"I just wanted to check-in one last time, before I got up there. Cell coverage will probably be lousy. You've got the number to the camp office, in case you need to reach me for anything." Translation: In case there's any change in John's condition.

"Got it right here. But sweetheart, I really want you to give this a chance. Embrace the whole camp experience. You used to have such fun up there. Unplugging from things will be good for you."

Unplugging. An unfortunate word choice.

Hudson closed his eyes as his brain conjured the tone of a flatlining heart monitor. His hand fisted around the fork. "Yeah. I'll try."

By the time he got off the phone, he'd lost whatever appetite he'd had for the pie. He ate it anyway, a mechanical shoveling in of food that had become habit the past few months. Food was necessary fuel, whether you tasted it or not. Leaving some cash on the table to pay his bill, he gassed up the Jeep. Then, remembering the promise to his mother, he bought a couple of packs of Twizzlers for nostalgia's sake and got back on the road to camp.

The bus crowd had cleared out. A lone blonde with a ponytail sat at the registration table. She looked up at his approach and broke into a grin. "Why Hudson Lowell. Didn't you grow up nice?"

"Don't know about nice, but I grew up. So'd you. Heard you married Michael."

"I did. We run this place together."

"Suits you," Hudson said. Heather Hawn had been one of his first camp crushes, but she'd never had eyes for anybody but Michael Tully. She looked happy. The kind of down-to-the-bone happy that exhausted him just from looking.

She checked her clipboard. "You're in Cabin 16 with Charlie Thayer. He got here about an hour ago from New York. You're in Syracuse these days?"

"I am."

Seeming to sense his reticence to talk, Heather turned all businesslike. "Not that I think you'll need it, but here's a map of camp and our list of available activities. Dinner's at six, and we're having an opening night dance at the boathouse at seven-thirty."

He'd rather be shot. But he took the handouts and thanked her before turning toward the Jeep for his gear.

"Oh, Hudson, I'll need your phone."

"Sorry?"

"We're banning them for the Retro Session. This is a technology-free zone."

"Not happening, Heather."

"You don't strike me as the type who'd be addicted to Candy Crush."

"I've got family in the hospital. They need to be able to reach me if things take a turn for the worse."

Her smile faded. "Oh, I'm so sorry. Well, keep it, then. But I'll warn you, reception is spotty, at best."

"Noted."

Charlie—whom he had dim memories of

from years before as someone they'd short-sheeted once—wasn't at the cabin when Hudson arrived, though he'd already claimed the right side for his own. The cabin was still rustic in appearance, but the Tullys had done quite a bit more than spruce the place up. Instead of the old-school bunk beds with room to sleep eight, there were only two twin beds with quality mattresses, already made up with real bedding instead of lying bare and waiting for a sleeping bag. Hudson shoved the one he'd brought beneath the bed. The bathroom was small, but functional, with hotel-style towels and travel-size toiletries. They definitely hadn't had AC back in the day. Curious despite himself, he headed out to see what else had changed in the past seventeen years.

The lodge was the most obvious difference. A grand structure of wood and stone, he'd read that it now housed five-star dining with an honest-to-God chef in residence, along with conference rooms, staff quarters, and luxury suites. Hudson guessed there was a market for those kinds of amenities, but he hoped there'd be some straight up burgers cooked over a campfire while he was here. He was more a pot of chili kind of guy, or he could go for a vat of spaghetti, served family-style around the long table at the firehouse. Not that he'd been doing any of that lately either.

They'd added a ropes course—a big, sprawling labyrinth of ropes and platforms. It was the kind of setup that looked more intimidating than it actually was. Climbers would be strapped into harnesses and attached to guide wires the entire time. Probably the liability insurance for the place wouldn't allow for anything else. But still, he'd check that out, at some point. Maybe he'd see if they had gear for some rock climbing, too. That kind of physical exertion suited his desire to push himself to exhaustion in hopes of maybe sleeping. He might not be out with his company, but he'd kept himself in top shape since he recovered from the fall.

The wooded trails crisscrossing the grounds felt the same, as did the long pier that branched off to the boathouse. Hudson could see racks of kayaks and canoes. He followed the pull toward the water. The gentle lap of it against the wooden pilings soothed his nerves a bit. He had definite plans to grab one of those kayaks and disappear. There were countless inlets to explore along the length of Lake Waawaatesi. He might even do some fishing while he was here. Fish didn't talk or expect you to talk back. He figured that made for much better therapy.

As he started to turn back toward camp proper, he caught a flash of fire. A woman strolled along the bank on the other side of the lake, her face tipped up to the sunshine, a gorgeous fall of red hair rippling in the breeze. From this distance, Hudson couldn't see her face, but he knew she was smiling. Everything about her posture suggested absolute peace. He found himself watching until she disappeared into the trees.

Shaking off the vague ripple of envy, Hudson decided to curtail the rest of his tour. Better to unpack and settle in before dinner, get a little quiet. He'd have to deal with people soon enough.

2

"WELCOME TO OUR RETRO Session at Camp Firefly Falls!"

Cheers practically raised the roof of the boathouse. Strands of twinkle lights were wrapped up the columns and around the rafters, giving the whole place a party vibe. The general jubilation of the campers added to the effect. Up on the little stage, Heather grinned from ear to ear. "Tonight kicks off two weeks of turning back the clock. We've got all your favorite, classic camp activities." She listed off several options Audrey remembered seeing in the brochure. "—with a few more grown up options thrown in." She gestured toward the bar that had been set up to one side of the dance floor. "My husband, Michael, is playing bartender tonight. We remind you to have fun and please drink responsibly. That said, let's get this party started!"

The sound system rocked out with "Here's To Never Growing Up" and people exploded onto the floor.

Audrey hadn't expected quite this level of chaos. She leaned toward Sam, raising her voice to be heard over the music. "Is this a normal camp thing?"

"Don't know about here. Hale River had dances, but nothing like this."

"This is a Camp Firefly Falls dance on steroids," Charlie said.

"Let's get out there!" Sam gave a little hop in time with the chorus.

"You two go ahead. I'm going to get a drink." With a drink, she'd have reason to stay outside the chaos and observe. No way would her legs allow for dancing. Not after today.

Sam gave her two thumbs up and dove after Charlie into the gyrating crowd. Was this what a mosh pit was like?

Audrey edged her way around the floor, watching and absorbing body language, automatically analyzing with her scientist's mind. It seemed a lot of these people knew each other. From what she'd heard, this was as much a reunion as a throw-back session, so that made sense.

What must that be like? To have friends you made as a child that either stayed with you for years, or who you could pick back up with after all this time passed as if it were yesterday. Audrey couldn't imagine that. She had friends, of course. Plenty of them as an adult. But as a child, she'd been painfully self-conscious, shy, and so far above her peers intellectually they hadn't been able to relate to her at all. She'd been weird. Awkward. A freak. It had been easy to retreat into her studies.

School was easy. School followed some sense of logic and rules, and her academic performance had delighted her parents. Continuing along that track had just made sense. College. Grad school. Going into research professionally had been a no brainer. Audrey had an aptitude, and, in the Graham family, ignoring that would've been considered a crime. Over the years, she'd quietly amassed a list of all the life experiences she'd missed out on because of a lifetime spent worshiping at the altar of academia—never with any clear idea what she was going to do with it. It was more as a form of observational research. After the accident, that list had become her Holy Grail.

"Hi there."

Audrey slid her gaze up to the guy who'd paused beside her. He was attractive in a clean cut, Ivy League sort of way, with the kind of confidence she'd seen often during her stint at Yale. The jeans and Camp Firefly Falls t-shirt he wore saved him from being unapproachable. She wondered where she could get one of those and made a mental note to track down one of the staff to ask.

"I'm Brad."

The correct social convention is to speak. Open your mouth, she ordered herself. "Audrey."

"Want to dance, Audrey?"

A refusal was on the tip of her tongue, but the music shifted into something less energetic. Something by Jack Johnson. Not a slow song, exactly, but something she could get away with not bouncing around to. Number thirty-seven on her list was *Attend a school dance.* This was probably as close as she'd ever get. She worked up a smile. "Sure."

Brad knew how to dance. That much was obvious when she put her hand in his and followed him out onto the floor. His grip on her was light but sure. Audrey forced herself to relax and follow his lead.

"First time at Camp Firefly Falls?" he asked.

"What gave me away?"

"The way you're watching everybody, like you're not quite sure what to do."

Audrey tried not to take offense at that since it was true. "I expected something a little more low-key tonight."

"Kumbaya and s'mores?"

Number fifty-four: Roast marshmallows over a real campfire to make authentic s'mores. That had to be better than roasting them over the burner of the gas range in her apartment.

"Well, I did have my heart set on s'mores."

"They have a campfire for that purpose every night, so if that's what your heart desires, we can absolutely make that happen." He flashed a too-practiced smile.

Was he flirting with her? Or just being friendly? This was one of those areas of human behavior she'd never felt comfortable assessing with any kind of accuracy. Uncertain, she gave a half smile and continued to watch the people around them. Probably it was rude not to maintain eye contact, but that felt too intimate. She didn't know what to say to this guy.

Brad's grip shifted. Before she could ask what that was about, he was whipping her out into a spin. At least, that's what she assumed he was trying to do. Her legs couldn't keep up, crossing over themselves like a pretzel, making her stumble. Pain shot up from her ankles, through her knees. Shock and an instant panic kept her from crying out. But his quick reflexes kept her from falling or from crashing into the couples dancing nearby.

"Whoops. Sorry about that. Didn't mean to surprise you."

Audrey held onto him, not because she wanted to but because without his support, she was pretty sure she'd drop like a stone.

"Audrey, you okay?" The concern in his voice told her she hadn't managed to hide the wince.

"I think I twisted my ankle." She hadn't, but it was the easiest explanation that would get her off the dance floor.

"Crap, I'm so sorry. Here, let me help you." He led her over to a row of chairs near the bar. "Should I find the camp doctor?"

She waved him off. "No need. I'll be fine. I'm just going to sit here a bit. You go on and keep dancing."

"You're sure I can't do anything?"

He looked so distressed at the idea that he'd ruined her evening, she relented. "Grab me a glass of wine?"

"I can do that. What kind?"

"Anything red."

He brought her a glass of merlot and, after much urging, returned to the dancing. Audrey let out a long, controlled breath, imagining the pain leaving with the exhale. Sometimes that worked. Sometimes it didn't. She'd have a date later with some muscle rub and the cold packs she'd shoved into the freezer of their mini fridge on arrival. She took a sip of her drink and relaxed in the chair. At least the wine was excellent.

Someone stepped up to the bar behind her. "Beer."

Audrey cocked her head at the word, not knowing why.

"What kind?" Michael reeled off several types.

"The IPA." There was something about that voice. It was deep, the kind of resonant timbre that soaked into your skin.

Come on. Say more than two words.

She heard ice shifting as Michael dug through the cooler. "You settling in okay? Got everything you need?"

"Yeah." A pause, as if the speaker were taking a pull on the beer. "It's a lot swankier than I remember."

Michael laughed and said something in return,

but Audrey didn't hear it. His response, the music, the pain in her legs, everything else faded as her mind zeroed in on the other guy. She *knew* that voice. Had dreamed of it over and over. Had heard it in her head, urging her on through all the grueling months of physical therapy.

Or maybe it was just that she wanted it to be him. Her nameless savior.

She turned around, hoping the sight of his face would jog her memory, but he'd already left the bar and was striding across the boathouse. He didn't stop to speak to anyone, didn't even acknowledge other campers were there. He just walked on out the door and into the night.

Before she could change her mind, Audrey shoved to her feet and followed.

Coming back to Camp Firefly Falls had been a mistake. But Hudson's mom had been so hopeful when they'd presented the trip to him—a surprise for the birthday he'd rather not have acknowledged. Some peace and quiet and fun was just what he needed. Right.

Sadly, only one person could give him what he

needed, and right now the fucker wasn't cooperating. Goddamned coma.

Hudson's cabinmate had somehow managed to convince him to show up at the mixer without earning a fist in the face. Charlie had the kind of unwavering good cheer that Hudson didn't know how to fight against, at least not without feeling like he'd kicked a puppy. So, he'd come and immediately wished he were anywhere else. At least there was beer. He'd lasted two songs before he couldn't take any more of the shiny, happy people or the blasting of the music. The thump of it followed him out to the end of the pier, but it wasn't so suffocating standing at the edge of Lake Waawaatesi. Just him and his beer and the night. No reason to let his foul mood spill over onto anyone else.

The sound of someone's hesitant footsteps on the dock had him tensing. Whether it was somebody from the old days or just a party goer looking to play Get To Know You, he wanted none of it. Talking was the last thing he felt like doing. He was already calculating where he could disappear to get the fuck away from people when a quiet voice spoke behind him.

"Excuse me."

Be polite, asshole.

Taking a breath, Hudson turned to find a petite redhead. The same one he'd seen on the other side of the lake this afternoon? She was a pretty little thing, looking out of place in her pants and flowy top amid all the camp t-shirts and shorts.

She stared at him for long moments with an intensity that surprised him, as if she were looking past his face to somewhere deeper. It was unnerving. Then her serious face lightened. "It *is* you."

Okay, not what he'd been expecting. "I'm sorry? Do we know each other?" Surely, he'd remember a face like that.

"I—no. Not really. You don't recognize me, do you?" She gave a self-deprecatory laugh, as if the very idea that he might was stupid. "No, of course you wouldn't. I'm not covered in blood this time."

That got his attention.

"You saved my life," she continued.

Hudson looked back now, really looked, mentally visualizing that face streaked with blood. Something about that macabre image snapped a memory into focus. "I-81."

"Yes."

He tried to remember the details. The accident had been about two years ago. One of the worst car crashes he'd ever worked. Even with the Jaws of Life, it had taken more than an hour to get her out of the car, and when they had…

"You're walking."

She beamed at that. "I am. The doctors said I wouldn't, but I'm more stubborn than they are."

"That's amazing." And he meant it. Her legs had been a bloody, mangled mess. Hudson couldn't imagine what she must've gone through to get to this point.

They lapsed into silence. As the moment stretched out from one to two, to more than a dozen, she knotted her hands in obvious discomfort.

"I just…I heard your voice. In there." She gestured back toward the boathouse. "And I remembered. I don't remember a lot of the accident…"

That was a blessing. He didn't know much about what had caused the accident, just that by the time he'd gotten to the scene, her car was more-or-less fused with an eighteen-wheeler and a mini-van and there were two fatalities. He'd been determined she wouldn't be the third.

"Anyway, I just had to see if it was really you."

"Guess it is." What were the odds that this woman he'd rescued from a mangled car with out-of-state plates would be here, now, at Camp Firefly Falls of all places?

"I never had a chance to thank you. I wouldn't be alive today, if it weren't for you."

Hudson felt something twist in his chest at the claim. "I was just doing my job. If it hadn't been me, it'd have been someone else."

"But it wasn't someone else. It was you. And maybe it was your job, but you did it damned well. You kept me calm and distracted, when I was in unspeakable pain. And you got me out." Something rippled over her face—a remembered pain? The fear?

He remembered her terror, barely kept at bay as her body went into shock. Remembered, too, the talking, talking, talking to try to keep her mind on anything else. The idea that that was still with her—and why wouldn't it be?—bothered him, made him want to do...something.

"Look, you got me out, and I wanted to...can I..." She shifted, dropping her gaze for a moment before bringing it back to his. "Okay maybe this is stupid, but can I just give you a hug?" Her voice was a little scratchy as she said it, and even in the darkness, he could see the stain of color in her cheeks.

Everything in Hudson wanted to step back. This was all way too close to *feeling shit,* and he had plenty of his own to deal with. But he also knew it would be a complete dick move not to grant her this one, small request.

"Sure." He set his beer on one of the rope-wrapped pilings.

Her expression eased.

He expected some awkward little dance, while they tried to figure out how to get past being basically strangers. Instead, she stepped into him without hesitation, sliding her arms around his waist and squeezing tight. She was a good bit shorter than he was, and her head nestled just right against his chest, somewhere in the vicinity of the heart he'd tried to shut off.

His arms lifted, wrapping around her shoulders, one hand cradling her head as he hugged her back because... He didn't know why, except that it felt damned good and nothing had felt good in months.

"Thank you," she whispered.

She pressed her cheek to his heart and sighed, a long exhale of tension that seemed to pull some of his own out with it. He stood with this virtual stranger in his arms and wondered if he ought to be the one thanking her.

3

HANKING HER RESCUER WAS possibly the most important thing on Audrey's list. To finally be able to do it, even if she couldn't really express what it meant to her, felt amazing. So did being in his arms. She'd expected a perfunctory squeeze, at most. But he'd hugged her back, and what had been meant as a simple thank you had turned into an embrace. Had she ever really let anyone hold her? Not like this. This whole thing had gone on way longer than she'd intended because...well, he seemed to need it. She knew grief and pain, and she'd recognized it in his face. If a simple hug would help even a little bit, who was she to deny him?

He seemed to register the weirdness a few moments after she did. They broke apart, an awkward disentangling of limbs. Audrey didn't know what to do. She'd said what she needed to say. She didn't really want to go back to the dance, but he obviously came out here because he didn't want company. Maybe she'd go find Sam and beg off the rest of the evening. Retreat to the cabin and ice her legs.

"Audrey," he said. "Your name is Audrey."

Something warm and fuzzy bloomed in her chest. He remembered her name. "Audrey Graham. I'm sorry, I never knew your name."

"Hudson Lowell."

"Nice to meet you, Hudson." After another beat of awkward silence, she started to turn.

"You wanna sit?"

The question surprised her. She looked around but saw no chairs. If she sat on the dock, she might not be able to get up again. But despite the risk, she didn't want to leave him. This man who had haunted her dreams for two years. The chance to find out more about the real guy was too good to pass up. "Sure."

Hudson retrieved his beer, toed off his shoes, and dropped down to the edge of the pier, dipping his feet into the water.

Audrey hesitated. "Isn't it cold?"

"Little bit."

Well, maybe this would serve the same purpose as icing. Using his shoulder for balance, she carefully lowered herself. He knew what she'd been through, so there was no sense in hiding the fact that she needed a little help. She pulled off her shoes and socks and tugged up the wide legs of her pants just far enough they wouldn't get wet. Despite the darkness, she was still paranoid about her scars. Knowing and seeing were two very different things.

The water was frigid and perfect, the coolness immediately starting to alleviate the ache. She flexed her toes and feet, slowly rotating her ankles.

He dangled the longneck bottle between two fingers, looking out over the lake. "How did you end up at Camp Firefly Falls?"

Audrey glanced over at him. "Because of you, actually."

"Me?" That pulled his attention back to her.

"You talked about it when you were cutting me out. I guess it stuck." She shrugged with a nonchalance she didn't feel. "The accident was a kind of wakeup call for me. I'd been putting all this focus on my career, practically since kindergarten—" Which was only a slight exaggeration. "—and I realized I'd been putting off actual living. Once I could do stuff again, I decided to start making up for lost time. I never got to go to camp as a kid, so when I found out they did grown-up camp and had a two-week retro session, I signed up."

"What is it you do?"

"I'm a professor."

Hudson gave her the side eye. "You seem kinda young for that."

She rolled her eyes heavenward, thankful that she was old enough now that not every single person she met had that reaction. "I finished my PhD at twenty-three."

"Seriously?"

"Seriously."

He digested that for a moment. "So, you were...how old when you finished high school?"

"I graduated a few months before I turned sixteen."

"Holy shit."

She shrugged again, wishing they could talk about anything else but how much of a freak she was. "I skipped a few grades." She waited for the intimidation or the interrogation about how smart she was. It was what people generally did when they found out.

Instead he surprised her. "That must've been hard. Being so out-of-sync age-wise with your classmates." It was an insightful observation and absolutely true.

"Yeah. I kind of skipped a lot of normal kid rites of passage."

"Hence camp."

"Hence camp," she agreed.

He tipped back his beer. "Well, for an authentic camp experience, you need a number of components."

Her mouth pulled into a smile. "Should I be taking notes?"

"Reckon you'd be good at that after all that school."

"True enough. So, the requisite components for an authentic camp experience?"

"You got your water sports, woodsy stuff, crafty stuff—I always avoided that like the plague, except for that one summer I had a crush on Jennifer Saylor and sat through macramé for two whole days because I thought she might notice me."

"Did she?"

"Sadly, no. *She* had a thing for Pete Zimmerman, who was a counselor-in-training at the time."

"So, you suffered through macramé for nothing?"

"Not nothing. I took home a real nice plant hammock to my mom."

Audrey giggled.

He continued to talk about all the different activities, ranking the stuff she really needed to try while she was here. And it was fun, sitting here with him, talking about camp, and flirting. She was pretty sure this was flirting. He told more stories about his summers at Camp Firefly Falls, entertaining her with various hijinks. He seemed to relax a little more with each story, until she could almost forget the grief she'd seen in his eyes earlier. She wanted to ask if he'd show her some of these places and activities, because she wanted to spend some more time with him, but that was still a little too far outside her comfort zone. Right now, it was enough to sit here with him as their toes turned pruney.

Behind them the dance was breaking up. People began to stream out of the boathouse, headed back to their cabins or to the nightly campfire.

Hudson looked over his shoulder. "Maybe we ought to call it a night."

Audrey hoped her disappointment didn't show. "Guess it is getting kinda late."

"Can I walk you back to your cabin?"

"That'd be nice."

He boosted himself up in a fluid motion that

had her wishing it was daylight and he was in nothing but board shorts so she could see the easy flex of muscle that enabled him to do that. That was definitely on her wish list of camp memories. Maybe later in the week.

Shifting, Audrey tried to lift her legs out of the water and realized she couldn't get up. After all the sitting on the bus and the sitting on the hard pier for however long they'd been out here, her legs simply refused to work.

Damn it.

For the last hour or so, she'd managed to forget she was damaged. He'd made her feel normal. Just a woman, chatting and flirting with an interesting, sexy guy. The last thing she wanted was to remind him that she was anything but.

HUDSON SLIPPED his sandals back on.

From where she still sat, Audrey burst out, "You know what? I think I'll sit out here a while longer. You go ahead."

She wouldn't look at him, but he could still see the flags of color in her cheeks, the hunch of her shoulders. Had he said something wrong? Mentally reviewing their conversation, he couldn't pinpoint anything, but hell, he was so out of practice having a normal conversation these days, how would he know?

Never one to push a woman, he shoved his hands in his pockets. "Okay, I'll see you around."

"Night, Hudson." There was something odd in her tone.

Not your business, he told himself.

He made it to the end of the dock before he looked back. She was dragging herself backward with her hands, maneuvering herself out of the water entirely with her upper body. Hudson cursed long and low for not realizing she was having trouble with her legs. She'd needed him for balance to sit down. Why wouldn't she need a hand up?

He jogged back to her. "Are you in pain?"

Audrey dropped her face into her hands, the flush creeping up the back of her neck. "God." She still wouldn't look at him. "No. Not really, they're just...asleep." Her voice was strangled as if she couldn't bear for him to see her weakness. "They'll wake up in a minute."

Not so long as she was sitting on the hard pier. Hudson scooped her up.

Audrey gave a surprised squeak. "What are you doing?"

"Which cabin are you in?"

"Seven. You can't just carry me all the way back to my cabin."

"Watch me. Here, grab your shoes." He bent so she could reach them, then simply curled her close against his chest and started walking. She weighed more than she looked, but he was willing to bet there was a fair amount of metal in her legs now. Not that he'd ask. Either way, she was nothing compared to the hoses and firefighting gear he lugged around on a daily basis.

"People are staring," she hissed.

He'd noticed that and didn't much care, but at the distress in her tone, he skirted the remainder of the crowd, most of which was headed for the nightly campfire.

"They'll probably assume we're headed off to find somewhere private to make out. That's another common element of the classic camp experience. Everybody's nosy about who's having a fling with who."

Why the hell had he said that? Now he was thinking about one of those camp flings and taking it quite a bit further than he ever had as a teenager. Audrey was a beautiful woman, all soft and vulnerable in his arms, and she smelled amazing.

Knock it off, asshole. You've got no business looking at her like that. No business looking at anybody like that.

Audrey had no ready comeback.

"Do you have a lot of trouble with your legs?" Not the greatest segue, but he had to do something to get his mind off the mental images that were making his shorts tighter.

"Only when I've been sitting too long or when I overdo it. Hudson, you really don't have to carry me all the way. Please set me down."

He had a feeling she was minimizing, but he detoured to one of the trail benches and put her down. Because he could still feel her embarrassment, Hudson turned his back, while she wrestled on her socks and shoes.

"Hope you brought some more practical shoes for the rest of the week."

"It was a dance," she argued.

One she'd spent all of with him. Not dancing. But he didn't point that out.

He offered a hand and pulled her to her feet, not asking before he slipped an arm around her. She wobbled a bit but stayed on her feet as they began to walk. Hudson kept his strides short and easy, moving at a pace quicker than the crawl he wanted, to avoid making her feel like an invalid.

"You don't like to take help, do you?"

"If I'd taken all the help people thrust on me after the accident, I'd never have walked again."

"Admitting your limitations doesn't make you weak, Audrey."

She made a little growling noise that was probably meant to convey annoyance but came across as adorable instead. "Screw limitations. I'm here to push past them. I won't know what I can truly do unless I try."

"Which is admirable. But be smart about it. You've got two weeks to ease into things. Don't push yourself so hard you end up benching yourself."

Her gait began to loosen as they went. "You sound like Chad."

Hudson felt a twinge of something. That wasn't jealousy. "Who's Chad? Boyfriend?"

"My physical therapist."

The twinge eased. No, definitely not jealousy. Because that would mean he was interested. Which he definitely was not. He had no business being interested in Audrey Graham, or anyone else for that matter. He was a wreck right now. But he found himself reluctant to let her go once she was able to walk on her own. It felt strangely good to have his arm around her and hers around him.

Where was this desire to look after her coming from? Because he'd rescued her once? He wasn't responsible for her, and he'd more than proved he couldn't look after anybody properly.

He followed her up the cabin steps, watching her feet like a hawk the whole way. But though she moved slowly, her feet didn't hesitate.

She turned on the little porch, tucking a chunk of hair behind one ear. "Thanks for the escort, Hudson. And the conversation."

"No problem." He liked the sound of his name on her lips. Too much.

The moment stretched out between them, feeling strangely date-like, which was absurd. But he couldn't help but wonder what she'd do if he slid a hand into that silky hair and laid his lips over hers. Would they be as soft as they looked? Would her body go pliant against his?

Audrey stepped back, opening the door, and reaching inside to flip on the porch light. "I'll see you tomorrow."

Hudson blinked, shaking himself out of the fantasy. "Tomorrow," he repeated, though he had no idea why. "Good night, Audrey."

"Night."

He waited until she was safely back in her cabin before heading back toward his own.

Charlie would undoubtedly be at the campfire, so now was his chance for some quiet time. And maybe he'd manage to fall asleep before his cabin-mate got back. Or at least pretend to sleep. Tugging out his phone, he typed a text to his cousin, Rachel. It took ten minutes of hiking before he found enough signal to get it out.

What's the update?

Then he waited.

Three little dots appeared almost immediately. **No change. Get some sleep, Hud.**

Sleep. Right.

Not that he'd done any of that consistently the past few months. Even if he managed to push himself to physical exhaustion, sleep was no reprieve. The moment he closed his eyes, he was back in that goddamned apartment fire. And that was fine. He didn't deserve a reprieve. Didn't deserve to forget, even for a moment. Because that minimized what happened. He'd survived, and he hadn't figured out how to live with that.

As the familiar heaviness set in again, he realized that talking with Audrey was the first time in months he'd felt like himself.

4

AUDREY WOKE TO BIRDSONG.

Bird song?

She rolled over, instantly regretting it as her legs screamed. Cracking one eye, she scanned the wooden walls and screen covered windows. Windows that were open to the cool, early morning air. It was a cabin, and she was at camp.

Sam sat up on the bed across the way, a book propped on her knees, reading glasses sliding down her nose as she looked over at Audrey. "Who is he?"

"Who's who?" Dear God, she wanted coffee like she wanted her next breath. But coffee was at the lodge, which required walking, which required she do her morning PT so that she could actually use her legs. Damn it.

"The mystery guy who carried you off last night."

Hudson.

Sam set the book aside. "I mean, way to go for getting right on out there. But who is he?"

"It's not like that." Not in real life anyway. But the snatches of dreams she remembered said otherwise. "I spent too long sitting yesterday, and I was having trouble walking."

Sam's amusement instantly faded. "You okay?"

Audrey covered her eyes with her forearm. "Just embarrassed. Hudson overreacted."

"I saw him carrying you when I was on my way to the campfire—we have to go tonight. You're gonna love the s'mores. I thought you were going off to have a romantic tryst."

Audrey flipped the covers back and began to push through the stiffness and pain to stretch and loosen up her muscles.

He'd said people would make that assumption. But more in a matter-of-fact sort of way than in an I'd-be-into-that tone. Not that her dreams had gotten the message. In that version, he'd kissed her goodnight, taking her mouth with the same un-hesitating confidence with which he'd scooped her up to carry her back. Even the memory of that dream kiss had heat crawling up her cheeks.

"Sadly, no."

"It's early in camp yet. There's time. I mean, there's obviously interest there since you two sat outside and talked for *two hours*."

If the party hadn't broken up, would they have talked more? Audrey felt like she could've talked with him all night. When was the last time she'd met anyone interesting enough for that?

She pulled one leg into her chest, straightening her knee and pointing her toe toward the ceiling. "It's not that simple. We have a sort of history."

"Oh really?" Sam drew the word out to four syllables. "How does one have a 'sort of history'?"

Audrey readjusted and held the stretch, breathing through the pain until the cramp in her calf released. "He's the firefighter who cut me out of my car."

"Seriously?"

"Yeah." Her own, personal hero.

"How does that even come up in conversation? I thought you didn't remember much from the accident."

"I don't. But I remembered his voice. It's a great

voice. Sort of deep and rumbly, like the purr of a giant cat."

Sam pursed her lips.

Audrey felt her cheeks heat. "Don't look at me like that."

"Like what?"

"Like it's a weird thing to fixate on."

"I didn't say a thing."

"That voice kept me sane and grounded, when there was a very good chance I was dying. It stuck with me."

Sam sobered. "Well, I think the fact that he's here, now, is a thing. Sounds like fate to me."

Now it was Audrey's turn to give her the side eye. "There's no such thing as fate."

"You don't think it's weird that you're both here?"

"He's the one who told me about this place. He talked about it while he was cutting me out. I remembered. That's it."

"So, really, you came here because of him."

Had he been somewhere in the back of her mind when she'd discovered Camp Firefly Falls was an option? Maybe. "I suppose, in a roundabout kind of way, yes. But that's not fate. It's just... logical consequence."

"Logical consequence. God, you're such a scientist."

"We didn't all get our PhDs by analyzing the literary ravings of dead white dudes."

"Dead white *women*, thank you very much. So you, from your vaunted, rational science position, are saying you didn't dig the hot firefighter?"

"I never said he was hot."

"So, he's not?"

"No, he's smoking." The words slipped out before Audrey could think better of them. But why not? Sam would see for herself it was true at some point.

"I rest my case. Look, you came here to make up for all those experiences you didn't have before the accident. A time-honored tradition is the summer camp fling. He seems like an excellent candidate."

Audrey had no desire to analyze the way her heart jumped at that idea. Sure, she was here to push outside her comfort zone, but deliberately pursuing a guy? She couldn't imagine doing something like that. She was too awkward, too cerebral, too... something. Ignoring the faint whisper of *Chicken* in the back of her mind, she turned the conversation back on her friend. "Did you have a camp fling?"

"My first kiss was at camp." Sam's face took on a dreamy expression as she wrapped her arms around her pillow in a hug. "Jordan Marshall on the last night of camp, when I was thirteen. It was terribly romantic."

First kiss at thirteen? Audrey had been a senior in college before she'd crossed that bridge. And when the other senior she'd gone out with had found out she was about to graduate at nineteen at the top of their class, he'd suddenly gotten very busy pretending she didn't exist. She didn't want to think about Cas the Ass.

"So, what happened to Jordan?"

"No idea. He never came back to camp. At least not while I was there. We just had the one kiss. Helluva kiss though." She shifted her focus back to Audrey. "I want that for you. A helluva kiss. A superior make out session. Hell, a flaming hot affair. You deserve to live as much as you want while you're here. Whether that's with your firefighter or with somebody else."

Her firefighter. Audrey shouldn't like the sound of that so much. Hudson wasn't her firefighter. Her hero, yes. Whether he wanted to admit it or not. But definitely not hers in any real sense of the word.

Did she want to change that? And if she did, did she have the guts to try?

Audrey didn't know. Beyond their unusual circumstantial connection, he intrigued her. More, he'd treated her like a normal woman, not a freaktastic brainiac. Not as damaged. Even when accommodating her condition because of her injuries, she hadn't felt like he thought she was broken. So, yeah. Fling-bait or not, she wanted to get to know him better. But that meant she had to find him first.

Physical therapy exercises complete, Audrey stood and reached for some jeans. "Right now, the only relationship I'm interested in is the one with my coffee cup. Let's go get breakfast."

DESPITE THE HUNDRED or so other people wandering the grounds, Hudson managed to spend the day completely alone out on the water. He'd kayaked the full length of the lake, well past the bounds of Camp Firefly Falls property. He'd seen others out on the water but hadn't come close enough to speak to any of them. He'd even found a hidden cove to beach the kayak and string up his portable hammock for an afternoon nap. It had been nice not having any of his friends or family checking up on him, trying to poke without looking like they were poking, to see how he was. He'd forgotten how peaceful it was up here.

But he'd found himself thinking about Audrey off and on all day, wondering how she was getting on with her first day of camp. He hadn't seen her. In the privacy of his own head, he could admit he'd been looking. He hoped she hadn't suffered any lasting ill effects from whatever was going on with her legs, and that she could get out and enjoy herself the way she wanted. He told himself it was a craving for s'mores that drove him to the nightly campfire, not that he was seeking her out. The little bump of pleasure under his breastbone as he saw her sitting to one side of the fire made him a liar.

She was in animated conversation with some other campers. "It was *awesome!*"

He had no idea what was awesome, but the delight in her voice made his lips curve. Good. She deserved to have a good time and check some more stuff off the life list she'd told him about last night. He didn't interrupt her conversation, instead heading for the s'mores supplies. She caught his eye as he dipped a hand into the bag of marshmallows, sending him a sunny wave before going back

to her conversation. Sliding a couple of marshmallows onto his stick, he settled on the opposite side
of the fire, where he could covertly watch her as
she smoothly rotated her own marshmallows
above the flames.

She was so... Bright was the word that kept
coming to mind. Even with the hesitation he'd noticed last night, she was so thirsty for new experiences, showing a level of enthusiasm for totally
basic things that most people took for granted.
Who got that excited about paddle boating? It was
something he'd always found dull, but listening to
her talk about her afternoon on the lake, he
couldn't help but smile.

"Okay, marshmallow toasting perfection
achieved. There is no way to top that."

"Of course, there is. With chocolate and another graham cracker." Another woman held some
out and sandwiched the marshmallow goo between them.

Audrey took the treat with careful hands and
bit in, her eyes going comically wide as she started
fanning with one hand. "*Hot!*"

Her friend laughed. "You're supposed to wait a
little bit for it to cool off. Here, have some water."

Audrey washed it down, then almost immediately took another bite. "I didn't need the skin on

the roof of my mouth anyway. Holy crap, this is so much better over a real fire."

"Told ya," her friend said, smug.

Audrey polished off the s'more with a happy little moan that had parts of him thinking happy thoughts as well. His stick dipped and his marshmallow caught fire.

"Shit." Hudson yanked it back and blew out the flame.

Eyes twinkling, Audrey stood up and stepped forward, extending her hands to warm them. "Need a refresher?"

"Some people like them charred." He wasn't one of them, but she didn't need to know that. He popped the blackened lump of sugar into his mouth and chewed. "Good day?"

Her smile spread wide. The sight of it did funny things to his chest.

"Great day. I made pottery."

"Enjoyed getting your hands dirty, huh?"

"So much." She laughed. Someone called her name and she turned.

Everything seemed to snap into slow motion. Hudson could see her pivot, see her knee buckling, her balance failing, tipping her toward the heart of the fire.

He didn't hesitate. He exploded up, leaping

through the flames. With relief, he felt the impact of her body against his, their combined momentum carrying her away from certain disaster. He twisted, wrapping himself around her so that it was him who hit the ground first, cushioning her landing.

For an instant, he froze, his body remembering the fall as the roof gave way. Phantom flames licked him from all sides, and he could see Steve falling beside him, slamming into a railing, and plummeting down the stairwell.

Not real. Not now. Audrey.

Hudson shoved himself up, running his hands over her, checking for flames, for burns. Frantic. A dim, distant part of himself recognized he was kind of losing his shit. Which was the reason he hadn't been out on any fire calls in three months. He couldn't be trusted to hold it together.

Soft, cool hands pressed against his cheeks. "Hudson, I'm okay."

His brain short circuited, abruptly cutting off the panic.

Audrey was sprawled across his lap. As he focused on her face, she gave him a lopsided smile. "Well, I guess you can take the fireman out of the turnout pants."

God, yes.

It was clearly meant to be a joke, but his dick didn't get the message. It leapt to attention, ready and willing to burn through some of the adrenaline still pumping through his system.

He saw the moment she caught the sexual undertone. Those bright blue eyes went dark, and the pulse at the base of her throat began to throb.

And they were surrounded by at least a dozen other people.

"Dude, that was amazing."

"Are you *insane?*"

"No, he's a firefighter."

"Are *you* burned?" Audrey asked.

Would he even register if he were? "No." If he found anything later, he knew well enough how to deal with it.

They disentangled themselves. Hudson rolled to his feet and reached down to pull Audrey to hers. She wobbled a little but stood on her own, no apparent lingering issues in her legs.

"Why don't you walk me back?"

Which was how Hudson found himself on the trail, alone with Audrey a few minutes later. He was mortified to realize he was shaking. The adrenaline dump was a killer.

Once they were out of earshot, she touched his arm. "Are you okay?"

No, no he was definitely not okay. He hadn't been okay for three months. But he wasn't gonna talk about that.

"You're really okay?" he asked instead.

"I really am, thanks to you. Again." Her face twisted with chagrin. "I swear, I'm not normally that much of a klutz."

She'd nearly fallen into a campfire from nothing more than turning wrong. His heart still hadn't quite settled back to normal. He could too easily imagine the damage if he hadn't caught her in time. The woman needed a keeper.

They arrived back at her cabin, and he found himself in the exact same position he'd been in last night. Because he wanted to touch her, Hudson shoved his hands in his pockets.

Audrey turned toward him with a sweet smile. "Thanks for walking me back."

"Sure." Hudson wanted to maybe thank her for getting him the hell away from all those people before he made more of a fool of himself. But that would require admitting it had happened, and he wasn't doing that either.

She lingered, tucking a chunk of hair behind her ear. Her tongue darted out to moisten her lips.

She's waiting for me to kiss her. The realization slammed into him. He wanted to. And it wasn't just because of the lingering adrenaline buzz. He'd been thinking about it since last night, wondering if her hair was as silky soft as it looked and if she'd be hesitant or if she'd throw herself into a kiss with the same kind of enthusiasm she'd shown for everything else at camp. Which was stupid. He didn't know this woman. Not really. She'd come up here to have some fun and accomplish some stuff on her bucket list. The last thing she needed was to get dragged down by all his shit.

Hudson took a step back. "Glad you're okay." He ignored the way her face fell a little and told himself he was doing them both a favor. "See you around, Audrey."

Before he could change his mind, he turned away and disappeared into the darkness, her soft "Good night" lingering in his ears.

5

"SOMEBODY'S GOT A CAMP crush."

Audrey looked up as Charlie sat down at their table, a plate piled high with bacon and eggs in his hands. "What?"

"Hudson, sugar. He's talking about Hudson," Sam clarified.

Did they mean he had a crush on *her*? Surely, they meant the reverse, which—okay, yeah, she kinda did have a camp crush on Hudson. Not that it mattered.

"The guy *jumped through a fire* to keep you from falling into it last night. I hope you rewarded him appropriately for his heroics," Charlie continued.

Sam picked up her coffee. "I had two extra s'mores to give you time in case you did."

Audrey's cheeks burned as she remembered the look in his eyes. Even she'd recognized the expression of absolute hunger. If there hadn't been all those people around maybe there might've been...something.

"He walked me back to the cabin like a gentleman. There was no hanky panky, so your caloric sacrifice was for nothing."

"Opportunity lost." Charlie paused. "Unless you're with somebody back home and not free."

"She's available," Sam informed him.

"Then I stick to my original assessment. He at least deserved a kiss."

She'd been willing. But there'd been more than simple attraction and adrenaline-fueled arousal going on last night. She'd lain awake a long time thinking about it, about him. There'd been something in his eyes, in the frenetic movement of his hands as he'd checked her for injury. As if, for just a little while, it hadn't been her he was seeing.

She understood those moments of being not quite connected to the present because something from the past still had a hold. For the most part, she'd moved past the nightmares and the flashbacks, but she recognized someone still suffering. It made her want to be Hudson's friend. To earn his trust, learn his issues, and find a way to help him deal. And that was a very different thing from the uncomplicated camp fling her friends were imagining.

"I'm starting to see why you're a romance editor," Audrey said.

"I love love," he declared. "And it makes me a total hit with the ladies."

"Be that as it may, I'm pretty sure he's not here looking for anything of the sort."

"Don't you read? All the best relationships happen when you're not looking," Sam insisted.

Audrey sipped her coffee and decided their brains had been addled by spending too much time in fiction and not enough in real life. Or maybe not. What did she know? It wasn't like she was an example of "normal" in any category.

She opened her mouth to change the subject but trailed off as she saw Hudson walk in. Surely it was a crime in several states to look that hot in basketball shorts and a t-shirt. He moved with an easy grace and economy of motion that she appreciated on a whole different level since walking had become a thing she had to actively think about so as not to face plant on a regular basis.

Charlie let out a whistle and waved Hudson over. His gaze skimmed over them, lingering for a moment on her before he lifted his hand in a wave and began loading his plate from the continental breakfast. Audrey didn't think he'd join them, but a few minutes later, he was pulling out the chair beside her and dropping into it.

"Morning." Since when did she sound like a teenage girl, all breathless and excited?

Hudson grunted and shoved bacon into his mouth.

Okay then. Not a morning person.

Audrey searched his face for lingering signs of...whatever she thought she'd seen last night, but he was relaxed and focused on his breakfast. He'd shaved and his hair was damp from a shower or swim. Because she wanted to stare—he was a fine thing to see first thing in the morning—she clutched her coffee like a shield and changed the subject. "What's on today's activities list? I didn't look before we left the cabin."

"Didn't you hear? It's Field Day," Charlie replied.

"Field Day?"

"Yeah! It's a full day of relay races, water games, target games, tug of war. It's awesome."

It didn't sound awesome to Audrey. It sounded like torture. She was aware of Hudson's gaze on her as Charlie continued.

"They'll probably have us pair up or divide into teams."

Teams. Meaning competitions. Meaning winners and losers. Anybody paired with her would automatically come in dead last. She couldn't run anymore and wasn't coordinated enough to do anything fast. She was a liability to any kind of competition. Maybe some of the other activities would still be open. She could hide out in the pottery studio and play so Sam wouldn't feel obligated to partner up with her.

"Winner gets to pick the movie tonight. I heard they were setting up a projector on the side of the lodge," Sam said. "Obviously, we'll be together for girl power."

Audrey opened her mouth to make an excuse, but before she could get it out, Hudson spoke up.

"She already promised to be my partner." He shifted calm gray eyes to hers. "Remember?"

She had, of course, done no such thing. He'd barely said a dozen words since they left the campfire last night. Snapping her mouth closed, she looked at him, trying to figure out if he was messing with her. He just stared back, placid as could be, and took a bite of toast.

"Well you should definitely go with Hudson. Charlie?" Sam asked.

"All yours, sweetness." He shoved back from the chair. "Shall we go plot strategy?"

Sam wasn't actually finished with her breakfast, but she shoved the last couple of slices of bacon onto her bagel and rose. "Let's. We'll see y'all on the field!"

Like rats jumping from a sinking ship. That was fine. She didn't much want to have this conversation with an audience.

Audrey waited until they left to speak. "You don't have to do this. I can go do something else."

"Do you *want* to do something else?"

No. Damn it. She wanted to be included. She'd never been included as a kid because nobody wanted the baby on their team. But she didn't want to be the pity pick, even if it was by her camp crush. Maybe especially by her camp crush. "You'll end up losing with me as a partner."

"I'm not in it to win. I'm in it so you can be."

She hadn't known him long, but she felt confident that spending the day surrounded by dozens of other rowdy campers was not what he really wanted to be doing. He'd come up here for solitude. "Why?"

"Because you deserve a shot at the authentic camp experience. This is part of it. And...because it's fun for me to see you get excited about all this stuff." He shrugged those massive shoulders as if uncomfortable with the admission.

"Excited is a strong word. I'm not sure I can physically *do* a lot of this stuff. I mean, maybe if I had no time clock and no audience, but..." She trailed off, too able to imagine falling on her butt in front of all of camp. Not that falling on her ass was a new experience since the accident. But there'd already been half a dozen people by their table this morning to ask if she was okay after the fire last night. She didn't relish any other entries that confirmed her position as camp klutz, and she wasn't keen on advertising the reason why. She didn't want to become the entire camp's object of pity.

"Do you trust me?" He'd leaned forward when she wasn't paying attention, so the rumble of his voice came near to her ear. Why should just the sound of it continue to soothe her anxieties?

"What does that have to do with anything?"

"It's a simple question. Do you?"

She had a simple and instinctive answer. "Yes." With her life, certainly. Though bringing that up right now seemed like overkill.

"Then meet me at the soccer fields at ten. And bring your game face."

"WELCOME TO FIELD DAY, CAMPERS!" Heather's voice boomed from the bull horn from where she stood in the center of the soccer fields. "Everybody have their partner?"

A cheer went up from the assembled crowd. Well, everybody but Audrey. She stood beside Hudson, arms crossed over the number nine pinned to her shirt, mouth set in a grim line. He was starting to wonder whether pushing her into this was such a good idea. But he'd seen the expression of half longing, half regret in her sky-blue eyes when Charlie brought Field Day up, and he'd hated it. It was such a departure from the fierce determination she'd shown the other night when she'd talked about pushing her limits. So, he'd made the snap decision to be her partner and help her through the stuff she found physically difficult. He didn't think they'd win, but he figured he could keep her from coming in last place.

"We're kicking things off today with a camp classic. The wheelbarrow race. One partner will be the wheelbarrow, the other will hold that person by the legs and push. The object is to get all the way down to the orange cones, circle around, and make it back to the starting line as fast as you can. Partners, take your positions!"

Audrey took a slow breath and let it back out. "Obviously, I'm the wheelbarrow."

"Ever done this before?"

She lifted a brow in his direction. "What do you think?"

Okay, yeah. She wasn't excited about this *at all*.

Hudson caught her arm as she headed for the starting line. "We can walk away right now."

Those eyes licked with temper. "I'm no quitter."

The faint tone of insult had him smiling. "That's my girl. Let's go."

At the starting line, she looked at the other players getting in position and dropped down to all fours.

"The key to this is keeping your core tight and focusing on one step at a time with your hands. Don't think about anybody else," he told her.

"Got it."

"On your marks!" Heather called.

Audrey rose into a push-up, and Hudson couldn't help but notice the flex of muscle in her shoulders and arms beneath the tank top she wore.

"Get set!"

He grasped her by the ankles and lifted.

"Go!"

She took off, all but running on her hands. They edged to the front of the pack, neck-and-neck with two other teams. He kept a close eye on her, expecting her to start flagging any second. The team to their left went down in a heap. Curses rose on the air, but Audrey kept moving, smooth and steady as they neared the cone. The team ahead on the right fell over into a pile of giggles as they rounded their cone. Audrey didn't fumble once as they entered the final stretch and took the lead.

"We've got this," he said. "Just keep doing what you're doing."

In his periphery, Hudson saw a couple of guys closing in, the wheelbarrow guy eating up the distance with his longer arms. Audrey saw him too. Was she *growling*? Hell yes, she was.

"Push!" she shouted.

So, he did. She threw her arms out, reaching, bucking, until she was practically galloping on her hands.

"Almost there!" he yelled.

Audrey leapt for the finish line, tucking into a graceless somersault as they crossed to a shout of "Tie!"

Hudson squatted down beside her. "That was awesome! You were a beast."

From where she lay sprawled, panting on the ground, she peered up at him. "Wheelchairs are great for developing upper body strength and co-ordination."

He wondered how long she'd spent in one over the last couple of years but wasn't about to ask. Instead, he offered a hand and tugged her into a sitting position. "Ready to go kick some more ass?"

She turned to glare at their competition and narrowed her eyes to slits. "It is *on!* Help me up."

After her reluctance to even admit she needed help the other night, this felt like a different kind of victory. She wrapped her hands around his fore-arms and he rose, lifting them both to their feet. Audrey wobbled a bit, stumbling into him. Instinc-tively, he shifted to steady her, one hand going to her waist and brushing bare skin where her shirt had ridden up. Before he could stop himself, he rubbed a thumb along the smooth warmth of her flesh. Her fingers tightened on his arms, her pupils blowing wide. It would be so easy to slide his hand around to the small of her back and pull her against him—

"Good job everybody!" Heather's voice rang out over the cheers of the crowd. "Big round of applause for Team 4 and Team 9, who are currently tied for first place."

Hudson let her go before he could give in to the terrible idea that kept kicking around in his head, barely noticing the back thumps and fist bumps of congratulations. He was here for Audrey. But he wasn't here *for* Audrey. It was best he remember that.

If any hint of arousal lingered, she hid it well, throwing herself into the next round of activity. And that was just fine. It helped him keep his head in the games. Whatever trepidation she'd felt at the prospect of participating seemed to have evaporated. They lost their lead in the sack race. No surprise, and Hudson was grateful Audrey didn't hurt herself. The impact of all that jumping had to be rough on her knees. Not that she uttered a word of complaint. They made up for lost points in the bean bag toss. Turned out she had wicked good aim. With Hudson edging out the competition in the football toss, they were just clinging to third place as they prepared for the three-legged race.

"Which is your dominant leg?" he asked.

"Used to be left. These days it doesn't really matter." She tipped back a bottle of water and guzzled it.

Hudson moved around to her right side and

bent to tie their legs together at the ankles. Audrey was shaking as Hudson straightened. "You okay?"

"Tired. I'm not used to exerting myself quite this much." Her cheeks were flushed and wisps of hair clung to her damp face, but she didn't seem to be in pain.

He slid an arm around her, as much out of a desire to comfort as to keep his balance. "We just need to get through this last event, then we break for lunch."

"I never dreamed we'd be in this long." She finished off the water and glanced up at him through lowered lashes. "Looks like we make a good team."

"Looks like."

It was too easy to imagine her words meant more. Because they did make a good team. She was easy to be with. No pressure, no worries—well, other than keeping an eye out for her general safety. Their silences were comfortable. Yeah, if he were looking for a camp fling, Audrey Graham would absolutely be it.

"Teams, take your positions!" Heather called.

Audrey slid her arm around his waist. "Ready to annihilate the competition?"

Hudson found himself grinning. "I like the way you think."

6

THEY DIDN'T WIN.

EVEN with Hudson practically carrying her during the three-legged race, they came in fourth. They slid further in the rankings in the water balloon toss, and things sort of went downhill from there. Audrey didn't care. She not only got to participate, but she and Hudson finished a respectable sixth out of twenty teams. They'd had *fun*. Then she'd promptly headed back to her cabin, taken a scalding shower in an effort to beat her muscles loose, and passed out. She'd slept through dinner. Maybe there'd be popcorn at the movie. She wondered what the winners had picked for everybody to watch.

Halfway to the lodge, she realized she

should've put on more layers. The concept of long sleeves in June for anything other than blocking the sun simply did not compute. But she was already late for the start of the movie, and her stomach was making a bid to devour itself. They'd set up a screen on the side of the main lodge. An older Kurt Russell, dressed in clothes that should've stayed in the eighties, sat at a bar, eating nachos. She didn't recognize the movie, which meant it probably didn't fall into the category of funny or romantic flicks she preferred. Campers spread out on the lawn in canvas chairs or lounging on blankets. Several had popcorn and adult beverages. Hallelujah. Skirting the edge of the crowd, she looked for Sam and the source of the snacks.

"Audrey."

Following the sound of the low voice, she saw Hudson occupying a blanket a few rows from the back. He waved her over. Trying not to block people's views too much, she picked her way to him and lowered herself to the blanket beside him.

"Thought you were gonna be a no show," he whispered.

It gave her a warm glow that he'd been looking for her. She didn't know exactly what they were doing, but there'd been enough moments and long looks that she was certain he wasn't indifferent to her. Which wasn't the same thing as being into her, but she'd take it for a win.

"Overslept." Her stomach felt compelled to punctuate the statement.

"Missed dinner. Twizzler?" He offered her the open pack.

Well, it wasn't popcorn, but it was something. She plucked a couple of red ropes out and bit in, nodding toward the screen. "What is this?"

"Some Quentin Tarantino crap. *Death Proof.* Never seen it, but one of the guys at my fire house raved about it. Can't remember what it's about. So far it's pretty terrible."

Conscious of the other campers, she kept her voice quiet. "Aren't most Tarantino films all about drugs, violence, and spectacle?"

"Seems like," he conceded. "I figure some kind of explosion is imminent."

"What would you have picked if we'd won?"

"*Die Hard.* Or maybe *Jaws.*"

Audrey nodded and started on the second Twizzler. "Classics."

"What about you?"

"Well, at a place like this, it seems only fitting to pick *Dirty Dancing.*"

He made a show of rolling his eyes and groaning softly. "My sister loves that movie."

"Every girl loves that movie. Or at the very least loves Patrick Swayze's very fine backside."

"Did you have the whole lift fantasy?"

She laughed. "No. And Sam won't watch it with me because I'm too apt to point out that there's no way Baby and Johnny make it. She goes off to the Peace Corps and does amazing things with her life."

"What about him?"

"I think he dances as long as he can and then, when the world changes, he probably ends up in some kind of trade job. Construction, maybe. But he never forgot the girl who stood up for him in the face of prejudice."

"Not a romantic?"

Audrey started to stretch out, then changed her mind as a sudden gust of wind had goose-flesh rising on her arms. "I like romance as much as the next girl. I just don't look for it in real life or expect it to have a permanent happy ending."

He shrugged out of his hoodie and wrapped it around her shoulders.

"How gallant. Thank you." She slid her arms into the sleeves and zipped it up, just barely resisting the urge to drop her nose to the fabric to inhale his scent.

"So, you're a cynic."

"Realist. Happily ever after is an unrealistic fantasy. Life happens. People talk about happiness as if it's this static state of being, and that's wrong. Happiness is a mindset, no matter what's going on in your life. It's a continual choice."

When she shivered again, Hudson wrapped his arm around her and tucked her against his side. It hadn't been a calculated move on her part, but she wasn't about to complain. After only a moment's hesitation, she burrowed in.

"Is that why you're so happy?"

Right now, she was happy to be sharing body heat. "I suppose so. Research shows that people who willfully choose to be positive about their situation in life have better outcomes than those who focus on the negative. I figured I needed every advantage I could give myself during my recovery." She shrugged. "I guess the attitude stuck."

He turned his head toward hers. "I like the attitude."

Only a couple of inches separated their mouths. Audrey wondered what he'd do if she tipped her face to close the distance. Did she really have the nerve to do it?

On the screen, some woman was getting into Kurt Russell's muscle car.

Something shifted in Hudson's face. "Let's get out of here."

Her pulse leapt. She was inclined to follow him anywhere, so she nodded. But there was a strange urgency to him as he pulled her up and into motion, wrapping an arm around her.

"Let's go."

Laughing softly, she did her best to keep up. "What's the hurry?"

"We need to go." The deadly serious tone was entirely at odds with the little fantasy playing out in her head of being hauled away to make out.

"Why?"

"Because I just remembered why Rodney was raving about this movie and you really don't need to see it."

Behind them, Audrey could hear an engine and squealing tires. She stumbled.

Hudson's arm tightened around her. "Just keep walking. Whatever you do, don't look." His voice thrummed with command.

They'd rounded the corner of the lodge when the crash came—a horrific rending of metal that seemed to go on repeating long after it should've been over, echoing off the nearby buildings. The sound reached into her and twisted, ripping open memories best left to darkness. Her body whipped with the shock of impact. There was one, long, surreal moment of weightlessness before the second hit came and her world narrowed down to nothing but stunning, unspeakable pain, as her car crumpled around her.

HUDSON BARELY KEPT Audrey from hitting the ground as she dropped like a stone.

"Audrey? Audrey!"

Her face had gone ashen. The pulse in her throat thundered way too fast and her breathing was ragged. She wasn't unconscious, but she wasn't with him either.

Shit, shit, shit. Why hadn't he realized and gotten her out of there sooner?

He scooped her up, tucking her close against his chest as he tried to figure out where to take her. His cabin? Hers? Too far, he decided. What was close? He scanned the buildings, wondering what was unlocked.

The kitchen.

"Stay with me, baby." Remembering she'd said the sound of his voice had helped after the accident, he kept up a running monologue as he made a beeline across the grassy space, circling around until he found a door. Unlocked, thank God. It opened under his hand, and he pushed into the dark space. The faint glow of the emergency Exit sign lit the entryway. He turned into the kitchen proper and found an empty room full of gleaming stainless steel.

With nowhere else to go, Hudson sank down to the floor, his back pressed to one of the long counters. Audrey's small body quaked against him. He stroked her hair and curled around her. Talking. Talking. "It's okay. It's over. I've got you. Come back to the now, Audrey."

"Hurts," she gasped.

"I know. But you survived it. You came out the other side. Where are you now?"

Her teeth chattered through the shock. "Camp."

"That's right. Camp Firefly Falls in the Berkshires." Hudson wished he had a blanket to wrap her in. "Do you know who you're with?"

Audrey turned her face into his throat, a child-like motion that absolutely undid him. "My hero."

His heart pinched. He didn't deserve that title. Not really. Any of his crew could have been the one to cut her out of that car. And nothing he'd done since they got here was heroic. But if thinking that helped pull her out of the grip of the flashback, he wasn't going to argue.

At length, her shaking stopped and her breath evened out. He wondered if she'd fallen asleep.

"Thank you."

Apparently not. "For what?"

"For getting me away."

Another wave of self-recriminations crashed over him. "Not fast enough."

"Believe me, it would've been worse if I'd seen it."

"I'm sorry. I should've realized sooner."

"We both should've used the brains God gave us and walked away when we found out it was Tarantino. Enough said." She lifted her head. "Thank you for taking care of me. I don't think Sam was out there, and I really don't want to think about everybody in camp being privy to me having a panic attack."

Hudson couldn't stop himself from tucking a lock of loose hair behind her ear. Taking care of her was as natural as breathing. He didn't really want to analyze why that was the case. "Still hurting?"

"It's fading. I'll be okay in a little while."

"Think an ice cream sundae might help?"

She let loose a little bubble of surprised laughter. "What?"

"Well, you never did get dinner, and we're in the kitchen. Might as well make a raid." Maybe he could turn this night around and take her mind off what had just happened. "Middle of the night kitchen raids are a camp tradition."

"Think they still stock the same staples they had when you were a kid?"

"If there isn't an industrial size vat of peanut butter and an equally large container of vanilla ice cream, I'll be most disappointed."

Her lips curved, some of the strain leaving her face. "Let's find out."

They disentangled themselves and got to their feet. Audrey used the counters for balance as she made her way to the doorway. Hudson itched to set her on one of them so he could do all the work, but maybe it was good for her to move. She reached for a light switch.

"Stop! Lights off for a kitchen raid." He dug out his phone and switched on the flashlight app.

"Hey! That's contraband. We're supposed to be cell phone free these two weeks."

"I'm a rebel." He didn't want to get into his reasons for keeping his phone. Moving over to join her, they made their way to the commercial freezer and tugged it open. "Bingo." Hudson hauled out the giant tub of vanilla ice cream.

"I'll check the fridge for toppings." She opened the next door and ducked her head inside, while he searched the pantry shelves.

Ten minutes later, they'd turned up all the fixings for ice cream sundaes.

"One scoop or two?" he asked.

"Three. No dinner, remember?"

"A woman after my own heart." Hudson scooped three blobs of ice cream into bowls for each of them.

Audrey followed with chocolate syrup, peanut butter, and whipped cream. She topped them off with chopped pecans. "Cherry?"

"I do not like fruit with my ice cream."

"It's not my favorite, but I feel like sundaes are a personal challenge to try to tie the cherry stem into a knot with my tongue." She bit the cherry off and popped the stem into her mouth.

"Ever managed it?"

Holding up a finger, she worked her mouth,

face twisted in fierce concentration. Amused, he picked up his sundae and spooned up a bite as he watched. A couple of minutes later, she opened her mouth and plucked out a knotted cherry stem.

The thought of how agile her tongue had to be to pull that off had his brain veering back into dangerous territory. He was grateful for the relative darkness as he gave a slow clap. "I'm impressed."

Audrey boosted herself up onto the counter and picked up her own sundae, digging in with gusto. "God. This is so good."

"Middle of the night ice cream usually is."

"I'm glad you thought of it. And I'm glad you're a nice enough guy to be trying to pretend you aren't doomed to see me at my worst."

"I don't always see you at your worst."

"That's not *all* you've seen," she conceded. "But you met me when I was broken and on the verge of dying. You rescued me from falling into a fire because of my own klutziness. And you've just masterfully handled a total flashback to the accident. I have not managed to present my best face with you."

"I like your face." The words were out before he could think better of them. But what the hell? It was true. "And there's no shame in any of those things. The accident wasn't your fault. The fact that your legs don't always cooperate isn't your fault—and, the fact that they cooperate at all is a testament to how much you've busted your ass. And I know exactly what it's like to be dragged into memories of the worst day of your life." Damn it. He hadn't meant to say that either. She was too easy to talk to.

"For what it's worth, I like your face, too."

She wasn't going to ask. Something in his chest unclenched at that realization, and he found himself smiling.

Hudson scooped up more ice cream. "So, what's on the docket tomorrow?"

"I was thinking maybe ziplining. I always wanted to go, and the system they have set up here is supposed to be pretty awesome."

"You up to that after today?"

"I think so. The pain and stiffness are worse if I stop moving."

"Okay then. I'll meet you there after breakfast."

Audrey angled her head, studying him in that intent way she had. "Why?"

Because he liked her. Because he wanted to keep her safe, so she could enjoy her time here at camp. And because when he was with her, he didn't feel quite so shitty about himself. But he didn't say any of that. "Because I haven't been zip-plining in nearly twenty years, and it sounds like fun."

She smiled another one of those sunrise smiles that made his chest go tight. "Okay then. See you after breakfast."

7

"Soooo, YOU AND HUDSON disappeared awfully fast from the movie last night," Sam observed.

And then I promptly lost my shit. But Audrey wasn't about to talk about that. The more mental distance she could put between herself and last night's flashback, the better. "It's not what you think. We just decided to do a kitchen raid since I slept through dinner. The movie was shitty anyway."

"You should've come and joined us for poker in the boathouse," Charlie said.

"Next time."

Sam narrowed her eyes. "You okay? You seem a little peaked this morning."

"Fine. Just tired. Didn't sleep well. There's a reason our moms wouldn't let us have giant ice cream sundaes for dinner right before bed." *Right. Let's blame it on the sugar.*

"If ice cream is the only thing you topped with whipped cream last night, then you and Hud need lessons in how this whole fling thing is supposed to work," Charlie announced.

"We're not having a fling." And after last night, the likelihood that they ever would seemed minuscule. Was she doomed to always show her absolute worst to this man?

"That's a damned shame. You two throw off sparks every time you get within ten feet of each other," Sam observed.

Yeah. Yeah it was. Tired of the discussion, Audrey drained the last of her coffee and shoved back from the table. "Well, at the risk of encouraging your romantic delusions, I'm bidding you both good day. I'm meeting Hudson at the zipline this morning."

"Oooo," they chorused.

Audrey rolled her eyes, hearing a faint sing-song of "Audrey and Hudson sitting in a tree..." as she pushed out of the dining hall. She couldn't decide if she was annoyed or amused.

He was waiting at the head of the zipline trail,

dressed in cargo shorts and a navy SFD t-shirt. The stretch of cotton across his broad shoulders had her mouth watering. Just the sight of him had last night's horror fading.

His lips quirked in a half-smile as he saw her. "Morning."

That voice. Dear God. There was an extra layer of growl to the rumble this morning, and added to the stubble darkening his jaw, she couldn't help but think about what it'd be like to hear that voice in bed, maybe with that stubble rubbing against more sensitive parts.

Audrey slammed the door on that thought and sucked in an unnecessarily large lungful of crisp, morning air. "Hi." *Brilliant conversationalist, Graham. How dare he not throw himself directly at your feet?*

"You ready for this?"

For just a moment, she forgot what she was here for. Was she ready to say to hell with caution and pursue him? Her brain said hell no. Her lady parts were screaming, "Move over sister!" Then she remembered. Ziplining. They were here to go flying through trees together.

"As I'll ever be." Even she didn't know which question she was answering.

"Scared?"

Terrified. "Maybe a little nervous."

He smiled like he knew she was lying and gestured to the trail. "After you."

A part of her wanted to slip her hand into his, like a giddy teenager on a first date. Instead she started walking.

He fell into step beside her. "Nothing to worry about. You'll be strapped into a safety harness the whole time. You don't even have to hold on."

Oh, but she wanted to hold on. To him.

What is the matter with me? She'd never in her life had a conversation where everything sounded like a double-entendre. Never had a conversation where she couldn't keep her mind off sex. She'd had sex and hadn't been all that impressed with it, so the lack of it since the accident hadn't even really registered. Not until now.

He's an excellent specimen of a man. Big. Muscular. Virile. And you've got a little hero worship going on. Why wouldn't you? He's done nothing but repeatedly rescue you since you met. You're just a slave to biology. That's all. It means you're a healthy, adult female. That should be a comfort.

It wasn't.

"Audrey?"

She realized they'd stopped at a little gear hut, and Hudson had been talking to her. "Hmm?"

"You okay?"

"Woolgathering. I'm sorry. You were saying?"

He held out a bright red helmet. "Try this one on for size."

She put it on. With expert fingers, he checked the fit, snapping and adjusting straps until the thing fit properly. "You do this a lot?"

"Ziplining, no. But rock climbing, yes. And search and rescue training. A lot of the equipment is very similar. Here, let's get you harnessed up." He accepted a harness from the girl manning the hut and bent low, holding it out so Audrey could step into it. "Just put your legs through here."

She balanced on his shoulder and put one foot through, then the other, proud she didn't wobble. She'd done extra stretches this morning to make sure she was as limber as possible. As thrilling as his rescue had been the other night, the realities of her continued limitations and klutziness made her paranoid about the necessity for a repeat. "I thought you were part of a city fire department."

"I am. But I'm certified for search and rescue. Sometimes I get called out for work elsewhere." He pulled the harness up to her hips and started adjusting those straps.

Audrey tried not to think too much about the

proximity of his hands as they tightened and tugged, jerking her hips around a bit as he worked.

"All set. You wanna check my work?"

The staff woman nodded and looked Audrey over while Hudson put on his own harness and helmet. "Just right. Both of you."

They followed her over to a wooden platform. At the ladder, Audrey tipped her head back and looked up and up. She hadn't counted on a ladder.

"You go up first," Hudson said. "I'll be right behind you. If you slip, I'll be right there to catch you."

Audrey appreciated that he could say that without sounding patronizing. She blew out a breath. "Okay. Up we go."

The staff woman went first, clambering up with the agility of a monkey. Audrey ignored that, and put one foot on the ladder.

Hudson was right at her shoulder, close enough that if she leaned back, just an inch or two, she'd be touching him. "Just take your time. I'm right here." He gripped the ladder on either side of her. But instead of making her feel crowded, it made her feel safe.

She began to climb. It took an embarrassingly long time, but she didn't slip, didn't have any trouble with her footing. And if she enjoyed the periodic brush of Hudson's body against hers as he climbed up almost directly behind her, who could blame her for that?

The staff woman helped her up onto the platform and immediately snapped the safety line onto the rigging above their heads. Even so, Audrey scooted to the massive post in the center and wrapped her arms around it. "Holy crap, this is high."

Hudson leapt lightly onto the platform behind her. "You got a heights thing?"

"It's never come up before." Why would it? She'd never been outdoorsy and the highest she'd been was at mountain overlooks or skyscrapers, behind nice, solid safety railings and windows.

"You're gonna be just fine. Taylor here has you all tied in."

"Can you maybe go first?" There was only a little bit of squeak to her voice.

"Sure can."

Taylor attached him to the zipline.

"Now here's how this works. You're going to step off the edge here."

Audrey's stomach dipped as she glanced toward the ground far below, then quickly pulled her gaze back up.

"Look at me. Just at me," Hudson ordered.

Audrey did as he asked, focusing on those calm, dark gray eyes, and felt herself settle.

"You'll feel just a little dip as the line takes your weight. Then you're just gonna slide down. You might twist a bit in the wind, depending on your balance. But you won't fall, and you won't hit anything. They keep all this ruthlessly maintained. At the other end, there will be a ramp angling up to the top of the next platform. You'll slow down as you get there and hit the ramp running, then slow your own momentum from there. The center pole the line is attached to will be wrapped in padding if you don't slow down fast enough, and I'll be right there waiting. Okay?"

It was the same soothing tone he'd used on her at the accident site. Telling her everything would be okay. And it had been. This was nothing compared to that.

"Okay. See you on the other side."

He flashed a grin at her in an unexpectedly boyish burst of excitement. "I'll be waiting." Then he stepped off the platform, backward.

His whoop echoed through the trees as the zipper thing carried him away from her. Before he left her sight, she saw him swing his legs up, wrapping them around the center line so he was flying upside down.

"Yeah, don't do that," Taylor told her.

"Don't worry. I won't!"

"You ready?"

Hudson would be waiting.

"Yeah."

"One, two…"

On three, Audrey stepped off the platform. She let out a little shriek at the momentary sensation of falling before the line caught. Then she was flying through the air, the trees zipping by. And it was *thrilling!* The forest opened up around her and she realized she was zooming across a little valley. It stretched out below her, pretty as a postcard before more woods swallowed her again. In the distance, she saw the next platform, saw the ramp she was aiming for. And she saw Hudson waiting. Audrey was already pedaling her feet, searching for purchase as she came in, faster than she expected. Taking the sudden weight of her body had her pitching forward, into a stumbling run. But Hudson caught her, as promised, wrapping his arms around her and absorbing the last of the momentum.

Audrey's breath wooshed out.

"You did it!" He grinned down at her, his eyes sparkling.

"Yes, I did!" Adrenaline pumped through her

system, and it was the most natural thing in the world to follow the excitement and throw her arms around his shoulders, pressing her lips to his.

His mouth was warm and firm and tasted faintly of mint. And it didn't soften under hers. In fact, he didn't move a muscle—not to pull her closer or push her away. The shock of what she'd done rippled through her and Audrey froze. A second later she dropped back to her feet, her face feeling like a five-alarm fire. "Um. Sorry about that."

She couldn't look at him as she stepped out of his arms. He didn't fight to keep her there.

"No worries." His tone was easy, unconcerned, as if women threw themselves at him every day. Maybe they did. "Want to go again?"

Yes, yes, I would, but I wish you'd kiss me back.

But he was talking about ziplining. And yeah, she wanted to do that again, too. Not meeting the eyes of the staff member manning this particular platform, she just nodded and let him switch her over to the next line. Then, without a word, she jumped and hoped the wind would cool the mortification still flaming in her cheeks.

AT THE END of the zipline course, Audrey made excuses to get back to camp. Hudson let her because he needed the space. Neither of them had made eye contact since that kiss. He knew she was embarrassed, and he felt like a dick leaving the giant elephant between them. But drawing attention to it would only make things worse. It couldn't happen again. She made him forget, made him feel good, and he didn't deserve that. When she rode the golf cart back to camp proper, he opted to walk.

He'd hoped it would clear his head. But all he managed was several instant replays, where he responded to that soft, sweet mouth on his. Needing to get himself grounded, he slipped out his phone, chancing that this high up, he might have enough signal to check-in on John.

One bar. Probably not enough for a call, but he could still text.

Hey Rach. Just checking in. How is he today?

The reply came back as Hudson was cresting the ridge, bringing the central camp buildings into view.

Rachel: **The same. Why are you texting? You're not supposed to have your phone.**

Hudson: **You can always reach me. You know that.**

Rachel: **You're on vacation. Act like it.**

Seriously? Did she, of all people, think he'd be able to switch everything off and just go on living as if his best friend, his brother of the heart, wasn't lying, unresponsive in a hospital bed?

His phone pinged with another text.

Rachel: **He'd be pissed you're doing this, you know.**

Then he could damned well wake up and tell Hud so himself.

Hudson: **I love you both.**

Rachel: **We know. Love you back. Go play.**

Play. He'd done that for a precious stretch this morning. Focused on this place, this woman—both far removed from home and work and tragedy. He felt guilty as hell about forgetting, even for a moment, but Audrey's infectious enthusiasm was a drug he wanted another hit of.

Well, now he had fresh guilt to add to the pile. He couldn't shake the sense that he owed Audrey an apology. Not that he knew exactly how to say it. *Look, I'm sorry I didn't kiss you back the way I wanted. It's not you, it's me. My life is a mess, I'm an asshole, and you don't actually want to be involved with me.*

Right. That would make her feel better.

She was better off if he stayed away. He managed to convince himself of that for at least a few hours, but by late afternoon, he sought her out. Even if he'd mucked up the nascent friendship—or whatever the hell was between them—he needed to know she was okay. After the highly physical morning, Hudson expected Audrey would be hanging in the crafts hut or the pottery studio. He remembered how excited she'd been about getting her hands dirty. Instead, he found her at the ropes course, strapping on yet another helmet and harness.

Well, you go girl. He stood for a long moment, admiring her moxie. Then, before he could think better of it, he was asking if there was room for one more.

"The hermit emerges," Charlie quipped.

"We aren't all as social as you," Hudson retorted.

Sam gave him a long, speculative look, but not the *eat shit and die* glare he expected. So maybe Audrey hadn't said anything about the kiss. Considering the speed with which she was attempting to climb that ladder and get away from him, it looked like she was still embarrassed.

Ready to leap into action, he kept a sharp eye on her until she made it up to the first perch. Then he slipped into his own safety gear and went up after her. His greater height and reach gave him an advantage in catching up. Whereas Charlie and Sam went straight for the upper levels of the course, Audrey was being smart and starting with the easier obstacles. So at least her desire to get away from him wasn't overriding good sense.

He left her to it, circling around from the other side as she worked her way through each section. Only when she made it to the upper reaches, to the tougher part, did he draw near. By then all her concentration was on foot placement and hand-holds. He made it to the top ahead of her and waited, watching as she slowly picked her way across the net bridge. Far below, Sam and Charlie shouted encouragement, having already finished their run.

Audrey was trembling with exhaustion. Hudson could see it as she made it to the next perch. One obstacle left to get to the end. The hardest.

"You can do it, Audrey!" Sam called.

"I'll need a nap after this," Audrey answered. She took a moment to catch her breath, then stretched out her arm, reaching for the next bar. It was several inches out of her grasp.

"You'll have to take the leap," he said, not so loud that those on the ground could hear.

She didn't take her focus off her goal. After a long moment, she said, "Tried that once today. Didn't end so well."

So, she had heard him.

"Took me by surprise."

Audrey looked at him then, a mix of exasperation and disbelief on her features. "Really? You're gonna go with that?"

"It's the truth." But it wasn't the whole truth. "Look, this morning wasn't about you. I'm...dealing with some stuff." He knew he couldn't just leave it there. "Make it over here to the other side, and I'll tell you."

"Promise?"

He held up his hand in a Boy Scout salute. "I'm a man of my word."

Audrey seemed to consider that for a long moment. Then she nodded, her eyes going back to the bars. She was too short to make it easily, but it was clear she was about to try. Hudson readied himself to retrieve her if she missed one of the narrow rungs that crossed the chasm and ended up dangling from her safety harness. Still, he wasn't prepared when she jumped for the first handhold. He sucked in a breath. But her fingers closed around it, leaving her dangling, feet nowhere near the row of steps across the bottom.

Her legs swung, her arms straining as she lurched forward, reaching for the next bar. She grabbed it. Amazed, Hudson watched as she repeated the performance, working her way across the final obstacle as if it were a set of elementary school monkey bars.

There was nothing more for her to grab onto at the final perch. Nothing except him. He opened his arms, waiting to catch her, wondering if her trust was so damaged that she'd rather not finish than do this. But Audrey didn't hesitate, pitching herself forward the last few feet to crash into him. Cheers went up from below. Hudson stepped back, tugging her away from the edge, out of view of their audience.

He ought to let her go. He'd done the bare minimum and caught her. But his arms wouldn't release, and he couldn't look away from her big blue eyes. Her adrenaline was up again. He could see it in the thump of her pulse, feel it in the tremble against his body. But she wasn't smiling this time. Neither was he. Somehow his hand lifted of its own volition, threading into the hair at her nape. Yeah, soft as it looked.

"Good job," he murmured.

Tension drew taut between them, and he knew

he was going to kiss her. He shouldn't. But he'd damn himself later.

"Are you seeing somebody?" she blurted.

"Right now, I'm looking at you." At her fearless determination and refusal to accept limitations. It was sexy as hell.

"That's...that's not what I meant."

Hudson stroked a thumb along her cheek. "I'm not with anybody, no."

"Then perhaps we could have this conversation somewhere with a little less altitude. The way you're looking at me makes me dizzy."

He smiled a little at that. "Yeah, we can do that. You up for a walk?"

"Lead the way."

8

AUDREY KNEW THERE WAS a chance she'd just ruined her shot at another kiss, but she was pretty sure he was entirely capable of scrambling her brain and distracting her, and she needed to know his story. They made their way to the bottom of the course. Thank God there were stairs down from the top. She didn't think she had it in her to navigate the whole thing again to get back to the start. She'd probably overdone it again, but she'd *done* it—made it all the way from beginning to end, through every single obstacle—and she was proud of that. Hudson looked proud, too. Though, why should he? She was nothing to him.

He challenged that assumption when he took

her hand, after they turned in their gear. Sam and Charlie, predictably, disappeared at that, saying they'd catch up at dinner later and making all kinds of suggestive eyebrow waggles behind Hudson's back. Audrey thought he'd let her go once he tugged her away from the ropes course, but he kept his fingers curved around hers, connected, at least superficially. In truth, she felt more than superficially connected to him, and that was dangerous territory. Except, he'd come back, seeking her out this afternoon, despite what had happened at the zipline. In the wake of all his rescues, that had to mean...something. Right?

"I'm sorry about this morning," he said.

"Which part?" The question slipped out before she could stop it. But since when had she ever avoided asking the difficult questions?

"Right now, it's an even split between not kissing you back and letting you walk off embarrassed."

Well. That was more honesty than she'd expected.

"You said it wasn't about me and that you aren't with anyone. Are you in the middle of a divorce?" It was one explanation that had occurred to her as she hung forty feet above the ground.

"No. Never married. Not coming out of any other relationship either."

Okay, so she hadn't been unintentionally poaching in someone else's territory. Which left what? The possibilities circled around her brain as he led her toward the gazebo by the lake, her analytical mind taking what she'd seen, what he'd said, and turning over the pieces, trying to make them fit. As they stepped into the shade of the gazebo, she voiced her conclusion. "You lost someone."

His head snapped toward her.

"You weren't calm and collected after the fire the other night. It wasn't the fire itself, because you didn't hesitate. It was that you thought I was hurt. Since you've been doing the job for years, the only way that made sense was that something happened on the job."

Hudson's eyes narrowed. "What exactly is it you're a professor of?"

"Sociology. I study broader trends in the development, structure, and functioning of human society, not individuals." Though she'd taken enough graduate courses in psychology out of her own interests to complete a master's degree. "But I am someone who's been on the outside for most of my life. I'm good at observing people. You're hurting. You're good at hiding it, but you're hurting."

He just stared at her, saying nothing, for long enough that her shoulders began to twitch.

"What?"

"I'm just wondering, if I wait long enough, if you'll guess the rest."

"That's as far as I've gotten." She squeezed the hand she still held. "Tell me what's going on, Hudson."

He released her hand and turned away, leaning his forearms on the railing and looking out over the water. "I shouldn't be here."

"With me? At camp?"

"Alive."

Whatever Audrey had expected, it wasn't that. She moved up beside him and mirrored his position, close, but not touching, and waited.

"Three months ago, my company got called to a structure fire. Multi-story apartment building. Three of us were on the roof. Me, John, and Steve. We've been tight since diapers. Done everything together. School. Firefighter academy. Joined the same company when we finished. We were a unit."

She didn't miss his use of the past tense.

"Shit was getting dicey, but there was a woman trapped in a corner room on the back side of the building. We were trying to get a handle on the blaze, redirect it so our people could get to her. But things took a turn." Hudson closed his eyes, his face twisting.

Audrey couldn't stop herself from laying a hand on his where it curved over the rail. It was hard as iron beneath her touch.

"The roof collapsed on us. Steve and I fell through. I hit the top floor landing. Steve crashed through the railing and fell all the way to the lobby below. Four stories."

She felt her heart twist and bleed with all the emotions he wasn't letting into his voice.

"I was out of it from the fall. Dislocated my shoulder, sprained some shit. Didn't know which way was up. Probably would've tried to go down the stairs, even though it was too late for Steve. John came down after me. He—well the details don't matter. He got me out. But before he could get out himself, more of the roof collapsed." Hudson's throat worked as he swallowed. "The rest of the company got him out, but he sustained some pretty awful head trauma. He's been in a coma ever since." He turned toward her, and the grief in his eyes all but brought Audrey to her knees. "I walked away because of him."

She wrapped her arms around him, holding

tight. She didn't say a word, didn't offer false platitudes or "It'll be okays." Because who knew if it would? She just hung on, pressing her cheek against his heart. "I'm so sorry."

He folded her in, wrapping his arms tight around her and burying his face in her hair. She had the impression he hadn't had—or let himself have—any comfort. It was clear he still blamed himself. And instead of embracing his second chance at life, as she had, he'd shut himself off. That made her heart ache for him. He felt such wells of grief, and she couldn't fix it.

Eventually he pulled back enough to look down at her. "I don't know why I told you that."

He'd made her a deal, but Audrey knew if he really hadn't wanted to tell her, he'd have found a way around it. "Because I've also been through stuff. You were there for part of it, so you know. And sometimes, you just have to talk about it. To get it out."

"I'm a guy. We don't talk about feelings."

"I won't tell anybody." It was part teasing, part serious. She'd keep what he told her in confidence. "But it doesn't change the fact that you have to deal with what you feel. I don't want to make you feel guilty." No camp fling was worth that.

Hudson lifted a hand to her cheek, searching

her face. "I feel a lot of things when I'm with you. Guilt isn't one of them."

She arched a brow. "So, you feel guilty about that?"

He gave a wry smile. "Yeah. Then I felt guilty for letting you walk away."

Her heart gave a hard bump under hear breastbone. "I'm not walking away now."

"I should." But he didn't move.

"Hudson."

"Yeah?"

"Maybe you should just acknowledge we both need this." Because this thing growing between them—whatever it was—had moved well past just wanting, well past the simple.

The corner of his mouth tipped up. "Are you always this rational?"

"Usually."

"Thank God." He closed the distance between them, settling his mouth firmly over hers.

Audrey sighed into the kiss, relaxing against him when he pulled her closer. His body was hard and hot, but his mouth...his mouth was a sweet seduction. No rush, no impatient escalation, just a bone-melting assault on her senses. She'd never been kissed like this, never even imagined this existed outside the pages of a book or a Hollywood screen. Like she was the center of his world and he had an eternity just to explore her mouth.

When he eased back, she sagged, hanging onto him for balance.

Instantly concerned, he shifted his grip to better support her. "You okay? Are your knees hurting?"

"Nope. I just don't have any anymore. You dissolved them."

The rumble of his chuckle felt delicious. "You're good for my ego."

Audrey had a feeling he'd be good for her everything. And that was just a little bit terrifying. She turned her focus back to stiffening her legs so she wasn't hanging onto Hudson like a limp noodle. Now that she thought about it, the exhaustion from her day's exertion was starting to make itself felt. She hadn't been kidding about needing a rest earlier.

As if reading her mind, he wrapped an arm around her waist. "How about we find one of those two-person hammocks and take a little nap?"

Snuggling up against that big, warm body and snoozing? "That sounds...perfect."

HUDSON DIDN'T KNOW QUITE how it had happened, but he was smack dab in the middle of a camp fling. Well, okay, he knew how. He'd kissed Audrey and quickly discovered one taste would never be enough. But he didn't know how he'd gotten to a place where he wasn't beating himself up about that.

There'd still been no change with John's condition. After assuring Hudson that she'd contact him the moment there was anything worth reporting, Rachel had threatened total radio silence if he didn't actually focus on his vacation. So, he'd focused on Audrey. It had been a blast. Somehow, when he was with her, his world felt—not okay, exactly, but less out of balance. And since they'd spent every waking minute together for the last three days, he was feeling—dare he admit it?— happy, for the first time since the fire.

"That's what you're wearing to go canoeing?" He eyed her cargo pants and long-sleeved t-shirt. "You do know it's June, right?"

"I also know I'm a red-head, and I'll be applying SPF 100 all day." She added a wide-brimmed hat to the outfit. It should've looked ridiculous. Mostly, he just thought she was adorable.

He had yet to see her in anything but long

pants. Fair complexion aside, he figured her legs were pretty scarred from the accident and subsequent surgeries. It wouldn't be surprising if she were sensitive about that. "And if we go in the water?"

"I've got a swimsuit on underneath. Although you assured me you're good at this, so I'm not anticipating getting wet."

His brain went off on a highly inappropriate mental detour at that. They were paddling out to the island in the middle of the lake. Total privacy. He wasn't taking her out there with the express purpose of getting her naked, but...the island did have a reputation. He was willing to bet that big brain of hers had precluded her from having quite a few of the more typical high school experiences. If she wanted to cross a few off the list, who was he to deny a lady?

"Hudson?"

"Yeah?"

Her mouth quirked, as if she knew exactly where his mind had gone. "I said do we have everything?"

"Pretty sure." He'd already stowed the picnic the camp kitchen had packed for them, along with a blanket and first aid kit. "You ready?"

"Always."

He loved that Audrey was game for anything, ready and willing to grab life by the horns. Such a different response to nearly dying. Then again, nobody else had died or nearly died because of her. Hudson shoved that thought away and helped her into a life jacket, lingering a little over the checking of the straps so he could tug her in for a fast kiss.

She was grinning as he set her back on her feet. "I like that part of the safety check."

"You'll want to keep a low center of gravity to avoid tipping." He handed her into the canoe.

She bobbled a little, then crouched and planted her butt in the seat.

Hudson climbed into the stern, taking up his paddle and pushing them away from the dock. "You hold your paddle like this—one hand curled over this little cross piece at the top, the other down here, close to the juncture of the blade and the shaft."

Not a good enough reason for using the word shaft, he thought, as his brain offered up a flood of images that had Audrey wrapping her hands around *his* shaft.

Hudson's voice was a little rougher when he spoke again. "You're going to turn your torso so the paddle side shoulder is forward and dip the blade into the water, perpendicular to the canoe. Then drag it back through the water in a long, smooth stroke." His cock jumped as he demonstrated the proper technique. *Jesus, when did everything about canoeing turn sexual?*

"Like this?" she asked, mimicking his movement.

"Don't come back quite so far. You want to stop each stroke about your hip. And you'll swap sides every few strokes. Try to use your core strength, not your back, or you'll regret it later."

After a little more practice, she had the technique down—and thank God. All this talk of shafts and strokes and proper rhythm had his board shorts uncomfortably tight.

They lapsed into companionable silence as they worked out their paddling cadence and made their way down the lake.

"Where are we headed?"

"Blueberry Island. Best place around for a picnic. Quiet, secluded, no cabinmates hanging around to be nosy and annoying. And if we're lucky, the wild blueberries haven't been wiped out by wildlife yet."

"Mmm. And how many girls did you take there to get lucky back when you were at camp?"

"I was fourteen when camp closed for good."

"So, you're saying you never took a girl out here?"

"Well, I might have brought Claudia Collingsworth out one night in the hope of scaring her pantsless with ghost stories."

Audrey snorted. "I gather you were unsuccessful?"

"Only partly. I got to second base, before a noise convinced her that Big Foot was coming to kill us both, and she ran screaming back to the boat."

She threw back her head and laughed, the sound rolling over him like a wave. He couldn't even be annoyed that it was at his expense.

"I never did anything so normal."

"I guess the age-gap between you and your classmates made dating pretty hard."

"I was, shall we say, a late bloomer. Dating mostly just didn't happen. Age-gap aside, nobody wanted to date the freak." She said it with the kind of ease that told him she regularly used the term, and Hudson found it really pissed him off.

"You're not a freak."

"You're sweet to get insulted on my behalf." He could hear the smile in her voice. "But I was. I barely existed on the same planet as my peers. The people in my age group were intimidated as hell.

The people who were intellectual peers either didn't look at me twice because they considered me a child or resented the hell out of the fact that I'd gotten where they were so much sooner than they had. I had no idea how to be normal. That's more than half the reason I went into sociology. I was trying to understand how society was supposed to work, to figure out how I fit. And the truth was, I didn't. So, I didn't date. Not really."

It was such a bleak picture and didn't at all fit how he saw her. How had she turned out so warm and open and well-adjusted? She'd just described an almost total lack of relationships with people her own age for a huge chunk of her life. He couldn't imagine that. Couldn't imagine the years without John and Steve. He couldn't imagine it now, and it was needing to face that reality that had brought him to his knees after the fire and kept him there.

He swallowed past the lump in his throat. "Sounds lonely."

"It was." She said it without an ounce of self-pity. Just a simple statement of fact. "It's only been in the past few years, as everybody else started catching up with me in their own education and career paths, that it stopped mattering so much. I'm old enough now that it's not weird I have a

PhD, and most people don't think to ask. Not that dating has been on my radar at all since the accident. The guy I was seeing when it happened rapidly disappeared, and I spent pretty much every waking minute in physical therapy."

"Wait a minute. The guy you were dating bailed on you after the accident?"

"After the first surgery. He wasn't prepared to deal with someone who'd be permanently disabled."

Hudson's hands fisted on the paddle. "I'd like to permanently disable him. What a dick."

"He was. He didn't love me, and I didn't love him. So, it all worked out all right in the end. I think that's part of why I fought so hard to walk again. Not because I was worried no one would ever want to be with me if I couldn't, but just as a kind of 'fuck you' to Lance. That and I didn't want to be dependent on my parents for the rest of my life. Don't get me wrong," she rushed on, as if she'd just insulted the Pope. "My parents are amazing, and I love them. But they liked being needed again way too much. They both had an epic case of empty nest syndrome when I finished school."

"I think a lot of parents have a hard time re-membering how to have an identity outside of being a parent once their kids are grown. That's probably worse with yours, since you'd have been so young when you went through college and grad school. I'm guessing they stayed way more involved than parents usually do at those stages."

"Did yours? Have the empty nest thing, I mean."

"Not with me. My baby sister was still around for another four years, and she was something of a hell raiser, so I think my dad was grateful to see her out on her own and thankful for whatever hair he had left at that point. Mom's a teacher, so I think she gets her fill of parenting still with her students. But it doesn't stop them from wanting to be involved or doing what they think I need. They're why I'm here. Mom thought camp would be good for me. Probably because it's one of the few things I did growing up without John and Steve."

Audrey was quiet for a minute, smoothly dragging her paddle through the water. "Has it been good for you?"

"You have." No reason to pussy foot around that.

"I'm glad." Her voice was soft.

Hudson wished he could see her face. They hadn't talked about what they were doing here.

They'd just been living in the moment, enjoying each other. Simple. Uncomplicated.

Except if this had been just a simple fling, he'd never have told her about the fire. And nothing about the pull he felt toward her was uncomplicated. It was all bound up in their shared history and a strangely compelling desire to protect her. To keep doing what he could to put that look of excitement and pleasure on her face.

Audrey cleared her throat. "Can I ask you something?"

"Sure."

"Could you—oh my God! Snake! Snake!" She shot to her feet, rocking the canoe.

Hudson immediately dropped lower, trying to counter her shifting weight. "You're going to tip us. Sit down."

"There's a *snake* at my feet," she squeaked.

"Okay, calm down. Sit back—"

She tried to step backward on the bow seat, rocking the boat until water sloshed over the edge.

"Don't!" But his warning came too late. The canoe lurched and Audrey tumbled straight into the lake.

9

"**I**T WAS JUST A little rat snake that had crawled under the seat to take a nap. They don't bite."

Audrey sent Hudson a withering glare. "It was a slithering thing *at my feet.*"

He wisely refrained from further comment, instead pulling a hamper and blanket from the canoe. Because, of course, *he* hadn't gone overboard. No, just her.

Soaking wet and irritated with her own overreaction, she unsnapped the life jacket and yanked it off, dumping it into the beached canoe. Now they were about to hike to...somewhere, and she was going to chafe all over the place.

"C'mon."

With as much dignity as she could muster—which was to say, none—she headed in the direction he indicated. God, she was embarrassed. But it was *a snake.* Hadn't he ever seen *Indiana Jones?* Didn't he understand the horror?

"So, you were going to ask me something?" he prompted.

Oh, hell no. No way could she ask him *now.* She looked like a total spaz. She was not about to still ask him if he'd be interested in checking off some of those bases with her, attraction be damned. But God, she'd been thinking about his hands all during their little paddling lesson, and then she'd stayed hot and bothered—at least until her unplanned dunk in the lake. She'd even been a little bit jealous of Claudia Collingsworth for having had those hands on her. Okay, maybe a lot jealous. Audrey knew how stirred up Hudson's kisses got her. She couldn't stop wondering about the rest. When Sam had tossed out the idea of a flaming hot affair, Audrey hadn't given it any serious thought. But now...

"Never mind. It was nothing."

"You're thinking awfully hard about nothing. And it's making you blush."

Damn her red-head's complexion! Couldn't a woman be embarrassed without announcing it to the world?

The little island was heavily forested, so she said nothing and concentrated on walking, so she didn't add tripping over a root or a hole or her own damned feet to her list of mortifications for the day. After all the exertion the last few days, that required a lot more effort than she liked. The hike to the center of the island didn't take more than five or ten minutes. It was a tiny island, after all. The little clearing reminded her of a fairy bower—which made her feel excessively romantic and stupid. Fairy bower? She was a scientist. A logical, rational professional. But the impression remained, with trees wrapping around the space in a way that suggested utter privacy.

Hudson flipped out the blanket and spread it out over the grass. "Pretty, isn't it?"

"If I were a Disney princess, I'd open my mouth to sing and small woodland creatures would scurry to the edge to pay homage."

He laughed. "You don't strike me as the Disney princess type."

"They were my guilty pleasure growing up. Intellectually, I get all the problems with some of the messages they put out there for girls, but I certainly never watched *Beauty and the Beast* and thought 'oh hey, Stockholm Syndrome seems like a good idea' or that I should change what made me me for the sake of some guy after watching *The Little Mermaid.* I just loved the stories and the music."

"Which one is your favorite?"

"Honestly? *Sleeping Beauty.* Which ought to be ridiculous. Aurora has literally eighteen lines of dialog in the entire movie. And *Tangled.* I guess I relate to the whole princess removed from the normal world. And the overprotective parent vibe." Why had she said that? It made her sound pitiful.

"I was much more into *Shrek.* An animated movie with fart jokes? It was great. Plus, Eddie Murphy. I love all things Eddie Murphy. I used to be able to quote *The Nutty Professor* word for word."

Audrey snorted. She toed off her shoes and started to step onto the blanket.

"You might as well strip down and lay out your clothes to dry. They have to be uncomfortable."

They were, but she didn't move.

"If you hang them up now, they'll probably be dry by the time we head back. Plus, it's shady enough here, you shouldn't burn," he continued, peeking into the hamper.

She still didn't budge.

"Unless you were lying about having a swimsuit on under there?"

She did have a swimsuit. A bikini. One that had once made her feel sexy. But that was before. She'd only packed it for camp because buying another seemed a waste of money, and she hadn't really planned on doing any water stuff anyway because she had no intention of showing her legs. Ever. They invited too many questions, too much pity.

And yet she was thinking about being intimate with this man. That would require exposing her scars—both literal and metaphorical. Could she do that? Could she really trust him enough, let him in that far? Hudson knew what she'd been through. Part of it, anyway. They wouldn't be a surprise to him. And maybe this was a good, safe way to test herself. To see how she felt about someone seeing her.

I can do this.

Before she could lose her nerve, Audrey tossed her hat onto the blanket and stripped off her shirt. She hung it on a branch, then unbuttoned her pants and slipped them off, too. But she couldn't make herself turn around to see his face. Her heart pounded in a sickening rhythm, too loud in her ears, and her skin prickled with more than just gooseflesh. She wanted to grab up the blanket and wrap it around herself, anything to cover back up. But she stood in the silence, biting her lip, until she couldn't stay quiet anymore.

"They basically had to rebuild my legs. Multiple surgeries and about twenty pounds' worth of pins, rods, plates, new knees... It's functional but not very pretty. Sort of Bride of Frankenstein. With better hair."

Audrey jumped when Hudson's hands skimmed down her arms. She hadn't heard him move.

"You know what I see when I look at you?" he asked softly.

"No." She could barely force the word out.

He turned her to face him, tipping her chin to force her to look up at him. Stubborn, she kept her eyes downcast, somewhere around his mouth.

"Strength. And that's the sexiest thing I can imagine."

Her heart flipped. She wanted to believe that, but she just...couldn't. "That's sweet, but—"

"I'm not lying to make you feel better, Audrey." He reeled her in, pulling her flush against his body until the truth of his statement nudged her in the belly.

"Oh!" Heat swept through her at the contact.

Audrey lifted her eyes to his and lost her breath. He wanted her. The huge erection was certainly a clue, but he could've been thinking about some hot model or a bikini car wash or any number of things that might turn him on. But he was looking at *her*, as if he wanted to devour her. It made her knees go weak. How was it he could see anything other than a woman broken?

Hudson cupped her cheek, sliding his hand into her hair. "Let me show you."

Had she spoken aloud? Before she had a chance to think about it, he'd lowered his lips to hers. They'd shared several kisses over the past few days, some initiated by him, some by her. They'd varied from hot to playful to sweet. But this. This was something else entirely.

He made love to her mouth. It was all she could think as he slowly stripped away her anxiety and embarrassment, leaving nothing behind but needs. She realized, as he lowered her to the blanket, that her sexual experiences before had been pale substitutes for what could be. She'd thought this kind of pleasure was a fiction, a fairy tale. The sort of thing that existed only in dreams.

If this was a dream, she didn't ever want to wake up.

His hands roamed over her, impossibly gentle as he skimmed those calloused fingers across her skin. How could such big, powerful hands be so reverent? They made her feel cherished, electric. And when his palms cupped her breasts, she arched into the touch, desperate for more. He tore his mouth from hers, and she whimpered at the loss, until he pressed his lips to the column of her throat, thumbs stroking her nipples through the swimsuit. Everything in her went taut.

Audrey tipped her head back to give him better access, threading her fingers into the hair at his nape as he kissed his way down to the little hollow above her collarbone and continued to massage her breasts. They were full and heavy in his hands, the nipples pearled tight and sensitive. With every brush of his thumbs, her sex pulled tighter.

"More," she breathed and couldn't even care that it came out a plea.

His fingers tugged at the knot of straps behind her neck until the bow released, then drew them down with slow deliberation. The sun on her bare breasts was nothing compared to the heat of his gaze as he looked at her.

"Beautiful."

He drew her into his mouth, circling her nipple with his tongue, and Audrey all but flew off the blanket. Hudson shifted, nudging one muscular thigh between hers, pressing right against her aching center, and, oh, that was better. Her hips began to move to the same, suckling rhythm he set with his mouth. Breath catching, she speared her hands in his hair, holding him to her when he shifted to the other breast. God, she was so close he was going to make her come, just from this.

"Hudson." His name came out on a moan.

He worked one hand between them, cupping her. Audrey arched into the touch with a cry. So. Very. Close. She widened her legs and bucked into his hand. He came back to her mouth, thrusting his tongue against hers as he rubbed the heel of his palm against her mound, and she shattered.

He held her through the shuddering aftermath, bringing her down with long, drugging kisses, and easy strokes of his hands.

"Okay?" he asked.

No. She was pretty sure he'd just ruined her for all men, and they hadn't even had sex yet. "That was...I don't...You're really good at that."

Hudson chuckled and the rumble of it shot straight to her still quivering core. "Not done yet."

"You're not?" she asked weakly.

In answer, he blew on her nipples, still wet from his mouth, and she felt herself stir again. This just might kill her, but oh, what a way to go.

He kissed his way down her torso, lingering at the edge of her bikini bottoms. She wondered if he'd pull them off with his teeth. That mental image caused a fresh flood of warmth. But he didn't take them off. Not yet, anyway. He ran a finger just inside the top edge. That only made her think of it going lower, deeper.

Oh yes, please.

But he didn't do that either. Instead, he kissed his way down her hip to her thigh, taking his time, continually skimming those gentle hands along her skin. As he neared her knee, she tensed.

He paused to look up at her again. "Still okay?"

She wanted this, wanted what he was trying to give her. She couldn't let her neuroses get in the way of that. "Yeah." But she dropped her head back to the blanket, not ready to watch him as he worked his way down the rest of her legs, over all the scar tissue. She'd just focus on the sensation of his mouth, his hands. Nothing else. She closed her eyes.

He straightened her leg, lifting it up, and she

waited for the feather-soft kisses. When none came, she murmured, "Don't stop."

Still nothing.

Was he waiting for some acknowledgment?

Audrey lifted her head to look down at him. He *was* kissing her, somewhere around her ankle. In dawning horror, she stared, watching him work his way back toward her knee.

Her throat went tight. "I can't." There were tears at the edge of her voice, but she couldn't stop them.

Hudson's attention snapped toward her, a frown bowing those masterful lips. "Audrey?"

"I can't," she repeated, feeling hysteria bubbling up in her chest.

He laid her leg down on the blanket, covering it with his palm in a gesture that was probably meant to be comforting. "It's okay. It's fine. We don't have to do anything you don't want to do."

"No!" She sucked in a breath and let the rest out on a sob. "I can't feel that. I can't feel you touching me."

WHAT THE HELL had just happened?

Minutes ago, she'd been moaning with pleasure, gone limp with the aftermath of a good, hard orgasm. Hudson had been good with that. Great with it. She'd looked so uncertain, so self-conscious about her scars, he'd just wanted to do something to make her realize how desirable she really was. Hell yes, he wanted her. He was still breathing and she was...amazing. Not because of that devastating intelligence—though that was sexy, too—but because of what she'd endured, how she'd come out stronger and so full of thirst for life. Those scars on her legs represented excruciating pain, both from the accident and the surgeries and physical therapy after. She still hurt, though she didn't let it slow her down. He had no idea how much being around him made her think of the accident, but he'd wanted to replace those thoughts, those memories, with pleasure—however much of it she'd allow. And now he'd gone and fucked it up. Instead of the pleasure, she'd remember this.

"Are you hurting?"

She shook her head, big, fat tears rolling down her cheeks. That just killed him. Hudson was pretty sure he'd rather be waterboarded than know he'd had anything to do with making her cry. He should've gone with his first instinct days ago and stayed away from her. This was just further proof that he wasn't fit to take care of anyone right now. But it was too late to turn back. He'd let her pull him out of his funk, let himself feel like a normal guy, who could have an uncomplicated fling. Now, they were in this together, and he'd messed up. He had to do something.

Praying he wasn't about to make this a thousand times worse, he stroked a hand down her leg, knee to ankle. "What do you feel?" He kept his voice calm, though his guts were tied in knots.

"I...nothing. It's just numb."

"Is it always numb?"

Audrey sat up, drawing her knees to her chest. She held the bikini top over her breasts, though she hadn't retied it. "I don't know. I still feel pain. How can I feel pain and nothing else?"

"Probably different nerves are responsible for those things." With all the surgeries, it made sense that there was considerable nerve damage. He stroked it again with firmer pressure, massaging muscles gone tense. "Can you feel the pressure?"

"A little."

"So, it's not so much the muscles as the skin. You're not feeling the surface stuff."

"I guess." She wiped at her eyes.

Taking that as a positive sign, he moved lower,

running his hands over her bare foot. It flexed in his hands. "You felt that."

"Yes. I couldn't walk properly if I didn't. Well, I couldn't walk at all. I'm not sure what I do qualifies as proper."

"You walk. That's a miracle unto itself." Shifting to her other leg, he repeated the process, touching, testing. The feeling came back somewhere around her knees in both legs. Very gently, he pressed a kiss at the threshold where she could still feel sensation. "Do you want me to stop?"

Audrey stared at him.

Hudson brushed his lips over the inside of the other knee. "We can get dressed, go on back to camp and pretend this didn't happen." Not that he was going to forget the sounds she made when she came at any point in this lifetime. "We can have lunch, as we planned. Or...I can keep going. I can remind you of what you very definitely still feel."

She was frowning, looking down at his hands, and he realized he'd been idly rubbing them up and down her scarred calves.

He stilled, but didn't stop touching her. "Sorry."

"They...really don't bother you, do they? The scars." She sounded completely flummoxed by the idea.

"No. They're a part of you—arguably an indicator of the strongest part—but they're not all of you. I want *you*, Audrey. The whole package." He didn't have a right to want her. She was the sort of woman who deserved promises and forever. Someone who had his shit together and could stand by her. He wasn't that guy. But right now, he could give her this. It had to be better than tears.

"Then don't stop." Throat working, she let the top fall, brushing a hesitant hand along his cheek. It cost her. Hudson could see that in the faint tremble that shook her hand. But she was taking the leap, as she'd done with everything else he'd thrown at her this week. He sure as hell planned to make sure she enjoyed the ride.

So, he kissed her. He kissed her like there was no tomorrow. Like there was no end to camp in a week. He kissed her until he lost himself in the taste of her mouth, the scent of her sun-warmed skin. She went pliant beneath him, relaxing, accepting—and it felt like a victory. Moving down her body, he used his hands, his mouth to coax her up again, steeping her in sensation. When he hooked his fingers in the waistband of her swimsuit, she moaned, "God, yes."

He peeled it off, baring her. She was lovely with all that flushed, alabaster skin. Hudson wanted to feast on it, on her, until they both found oblivion in pleasure. Skimming his palms up the outsides of her thighs, he watched her face as he bent low to press a kiss to her belly. It quivered as he edged lower, tracing her hipbone with his tongue. He expected her to close her eyes. Instead, she watched him, parting her legs to accommodate his shoulders. He settled between them, sliding his hands beneath her ass to drag her into better position. And he held her gaze as he lowered his mouth.

Audrey's breath exploded out, her body bowing in response to the slow lick of his tongue. She grabbed fistfuls of the blanket, gasping out his name. Her eyes stayed fixed on his, the pupils so huge, they swallowed up the blue. It was a shocking intimacy. More than the taste of her on his tongue, more than the feel of her heels digging into his shoulders. As if she saw that this wasn't entirely about her, but about losing himself in her pleasure, too.

Hudson couldn't look away. He soaked up every gasp, every sigh, every needy whimper. And when he pushed her over the edge again, heard her scream, he felt a surge of triumph.

Audrey went boneless, eyes closing at last. With one last kiss to the inside of her thighs, he shifted to stretch out beside her. Sleepy, sated, she curled against him, one hand reaching for the waistband of his shorts.

Hudson caught it, brought to his mouth for little, nibbling kisses. "No."

Her eyes blinked open, not dazed at all despite the lethargic tone. "But what about you?"

"This wasn't about me. Today is all about you." His raging hard-on would fade. Eventually. He wasn't about to take advantage of her vulnerability. She needed some time to settle and process.

"That hardly seems fair."

He stroked a lazy hand from her waist to her hip, enjoying that she didn't seem self-conscious now. "I promise, I enjoyed that almost as much as you did."

"What did you get out of it?"

His lips curved, and he pressed another kiss to her bare shoulder. "The satisfaction of a job very well done."

"Cocky. But accurate." She closed her eyes and rode out another shudder. "So very accurate." Patting his chest, she rolled away, tugging her swimsuit back on.

There were still shadows in her eyes. He wanted to say something, to ask—shit, he didn't know what. How she was feeling? If she was really okay? But he didn't want to bring up the whole thing again and make it worse. So, he said nothing, watching her. As they fell on the picnic like they hadn't eaten in a week, Audrey said and did all the right things, laughing and joking with him. But as they packed up to head back to camp, he couldn't shake the feeling that her light was just a little bit dimmer.

10

AUDREY COULDN'T SLEEP. RESTLESS, she retreated to the pottery studio. Probably there was some rule about being in here at night, without staff supervision. But she'd come often enough that she knew the ropes, how all the equipment worked. She wouldn't break anything. She just wanted some quiet time alone with the clay, to feel it beneath her hands. Switching on just a couple of the lamps on low, she perched on the stool and turned on the wheel. The steady whir of it soothed her. This was better than all the therapy she'd had after the accident. There was a distinct possibility she'd need a crate to pack up all the pieces she'd made since she got here.

She ached, in body and mind, both from over-doing it the last several days and from the discovery of yet another loss. There'd been so many in the wake of the accident. She didn't know why this one felt so huge, especially when she hadn't even known it was an issue until today. But it made her feel somehow incomplete. Yet another sign of being broken.

Hudson didn't think she was broken. And he'd certainly gone above and beyond to show her that she could absolutely still feel everywhere it counted. And dear God, how she'd felt. Just the thought of his mouth on her had her going wet and achy again. He'd given her the best orgasms of her life. She had the beard burn on her thighs to prove it. What did some lasting nerve damage mean in the face of that?

But he hadn't taken anything for himself. She didn't know how to feel about that. In truth, she didn't know how she felt about any of this, and for once her scientist's mind wasn't keen on analyzing it. She didn't want to be in this alone, didn't want to be the only one overwhelmed with feelings that were far too complex for a mere camp fling. She was in over her head, and she was deathly afraid that even Hudson couldn't save her from this.

The outside door opened. Audrey braced to

explain her presence to camp security, but lost her train of thought when Hudson stepped into the room, as if summoned by her thoughts.

"I thought I might find you here."

Had she become so predictable? Maybe. She'd been in here every day since camp started.

He crossed over to lean against a bench, looking mouth-watering and sexy in low-slung jeans and a T-shirt. Beneath her hands, the vessel she was drawing up began to dip. In an effort to save it, she switched her attention back to her project and said nothing.

"You okay?"

She jerked her shoulder in a shrug, keeping her focus on the quiet whir of the wheel and the clay.

"I'm sorry."

Her gaze flickered to his, and she managed a small smile. "For what? The two mind-blowing orgasms? I think we both know I enjoyed them." Just looking at him had her legs going loose and heat gathering low in her belly. She'd happily spend the next week in his bed.

Hudson shifted. She wasn't used to seeing him as anything but fully self-assured and confident. "No. I just...I don't know if I handled things the best way today, and I just wanted to see if you were okay."

He was so sweet, and he wasn't the kind of guy you expected sweetness from. She didn't know why he cared, but it was obvious he did. And that did something to her, warming a long cold place in her chest. She could get used to that. Which was foolish, as there was no room for a future with him. Regardless of what choice she made, neither job option was anywhere close to Syracuse. She wasn't even sure how she'd feel going anywhere near the site of the accident. Not that it mattered. They hadn't broached the subject of whether this could be more than whatever it was. Come next week, they'd both go back to the real world, and they'd both have to find a way to be okay with that.

Because he seemed to need the reassurance, Audrey worked up a smile. "There's no need for apologies. I'm fine."

"You're upset or you wouldn't be in here in the middle of the night."

She could've pointed out what his own nocturnal wanderings said about his mental state, but deflection wasn't going to work on him. "I'm not upset." Being upset with reality was pointless.

"I know you better than that." The irritating

truth was that he did. He understood her in a way few people ever had

But she didn't want to get into that. "Ever done pottery?"

"No."

"It's very therapeutic. Come sit with me. Get your hands dirty."

She didn't think he'd really do it. But after only a moment's hesitation, he crossed the room. She opened her mouth to tell him where all the supplies were located, but before she could speak, he'd dragged the stool from the next potter's wheel and sat behind her. It wasn't at all what she'd meant, but what red-blooded woman could sit in a pottery studio for a week and not have at least one fantasy about a Patrick Swayze in *Ghost* moment? So, Audrey went with it. "Give me your hands."

The hardness of his chest pressed into her back as he leaned forward, stretching his arms toward the wheel. She laid her hands over his and knew she'd be adding this to the roster of fantasies she'd begun to collect about them. She pressed his palms against the clay, deliberately collapsing the shape she'd begun in on itself. Starting over.

"I messed it up."

She thought maybe he was talking about more than the vase. "No. It was just a first attempt.

Sometimes it takes a few tries to get it right." Reaching over, she dribbled more water on the clay. "What does it feel like?"

"Cool. Slick. There are lumps, but I can feel them smoothing out under my fingers."

Audrey felt her own rough edges smoothing out as his warm breath brushed her nape. "I love that feeling. It's very Zen. Like no matter how much of a mess things might be, if you stick with it, apply consistent pressure and effort—" She cupped his fingers and used them to mold the clay. "—eventually things get better." Reaching to the center of the lump, she pressed a thumb in, guiding his hands to draw it into a bowl shape.

"Not everything does."

"No," she agreed. "Sometimes things are just broken." She brought their hands in again, collapsing the shape.

"You aren't." The fierceness made her smile.

Because she didn't want to do anything else, she let herself relax back against him, let herself have the illusion that she'd always have this strong body to lean on. That idea was as seductive as his very talented mouth. "Not in any important way, no. It's not how I think of myself most of the time. But sometimes something happens that reminds me."

"Being around me this week has to be one gigantic reminder. I didn't think about that before today." His tone dripped with a regret that shocked her.

"No. You don't remind me of the accident. Not how you're thinking. You remind me that I'm still alive. That I'm still perfectly capable of living a full life. I don't feel broken when I'm with you. Because when you look at me, you actually see *me*. Not the aftermath of the accident. Not the girl genius. Me." He had from the beginning. Turning her head, she met his eyes and swallowed against a throat gone suddenly tight. "I'm going to miss the hell out of you when camp is over."

"Likewise." He flexed his fingers to curl with hers. Neither of them looked at the clay.

"Hudson."

"Yeah?"

The words piled up like a logjam in her throat, but she forced them out anyway. "Tell me this isn't just me."

He shook his head. "It's not just you."

Something loosened around her heart at that, even as a part of her thought of the ticking time clock. They had only days left together. How could that possibly be enough? "I don't know how to do this," she whispered. "I don't know how to keep this simple."

"Because we're not." He dropped his brow to hers. When he spoke again, his voice was deceptively light. "You know how you survive a camp romance?"

"How?" She needed all the survival tips she could get, because she knew that walking away from him, from this, would be brutal.

"You take the time you have and don't talk about the end of camp."

Accept that this was time out of time and embrace it. If that was the choice, she'd already made hers. Maybe she'd made her choice that first night on the pier. "Okay."

Hudson angled his head slightly. "Okay?"

"Then I'm all in. I want you—all of you—for whatever time we have left."

OF COURSE, Audrey would choose to seize the day. Hudson should've realized that when he'd offered up the accepted wisdom for surviving camp romances. But there'd been a part of him hoping that she'd do what he couldn't and stop this thing between them before hearts got involved. Instead she'd offered him everything he wanted—for the next week, at least.

If this were a normal camp fling, following through would be a no-brainer. She was a beautiful woman, and he still had a pulse—currently drumming in his chest with anticipation. But this wasn't just a camp fling. They'd both already admitted to feeling more than they should, and taking this step would certainly reinforce that. There would be no going back, and he was positive that the week wouldn't be enough. But it wasn't in him to deny her anything. Not now. She was the only one who could still pull back. Hudson searched for the right words to get her to think about this one last time, without making her feel like it was a rejection. "Is that a good idea?"

She understood. Of course, she understood. "I've already told you I don't expect a permanent happy ending."

Maybe. But she deserved one. And that wasn't something he could give her—no matter how much he was starting to want to.

At his continued hesitation, she shifted, lifting her hand to his chest. "I'm not living my life for the future anymore, Hudson. I'm living it for the now. Because the now is the only thing you're ever guaranteed to have. You gave that back to me." She leaned into him, lifting her mouth a whisper from his. "Let me give this to you."

Right or wrong, he wasn't strong enough to walk away from this, from her. He started to lower his mouth to hers, then paused, holding his hands up. "Maybe after we wash off the mud."

Audrey blinked, then looked down where her palm had left a perfect print on the center of his t-shirt. Lips quirking, she slid off the stool, switching off the pottery wheel and heading for the sink. "Practicalities first."

She detoured to lock the door to the studio.

Hudson lifted a brow. "Here?"

"Unless *your* roommate is sleeping in someone else's cabin tonight?"

"Fair point." He ran through a quick mental list of camp locations for clandestine sex. Firefly Falls was too much of a hike and everywhere else he could think of carried too much risk of being caught. If they were doing this, the last thing he wanted was to be interrupted. Pottery studio it was.

He came up behind her at the sink, thrusting his hands beneath the running water, effectively trapping her. She squirted soap on her hands. Hudson pressed closer, nestling his erection against her luscious ass as he took those hands in his and slowly massaged the clay off.

Audrey hummed low in her throat and dropped her head forward. "This makes me wonder what magic you can work in a shower."

"We'll add it to the list." Taking advantage, he pressed a kiss to her exposed nape. "Personally, I really want the luxury of making love to you in a bed." And not just any bed, he realized. His bed. At home. It shocked him how easily he could picture her there, her hair spread out on his pillow, her body splayed out and limp from pleasure. But he didn't just see her in his bed. He saw her in his *life*. Cooking with him in his kitchen, laughing with his mom and sister, teasing the other guys at the fire house.

Audrey unzipped his jeans and slid her hand inside, wrapping those hot little fingers around his length, effectively wiping out his domestic fantasy. Hudson cursed, his hips bucking into her hand. Her lips curved into a wicked smile. "Oh, we'll find time for a bed. Because you've had your hands and mouth on every inch of me, and I really want to return the favor."

Whatever blood was left in his head drained south, as he imagined that pretty mouth wrapped around him, those big blue eyes staring up at him as she sucked him deep. Yeah, he'd perform whatever blackmail or magic was required to get them a bed. Preferably one where they wouldn't be interrupted for a solid twenty-four hours. That *might* be enough to slake this vicious thirst for her. For a little while.

"Hudson?"

"Yeah?" he croaked.

"You're wearing way too many clothes."

"So are you."

They dove at each other, tugging and tossing between desperate, fevered kisses, until they both stood naked. He watched, gratified as her eyes drank in his body, her gaze skimming down his chest to the jut of his erection.

"You're beautiful," she said.

"That's my line."

Nostrils flaring, she reached out to run a finger along the indentations of muscle at his hips. "I don't know what these are called, but they melt my brain. All I can think about is licking them." She bent and did just that, trailing the tip of her tongue along the groove from his hip on down to—

Hudson gently but firmly grabbed her head to keep her from moving further south.

Audrey looked up at him with a faint pout. "Turnabout is fair play."

"Later. When we manage that bed." Not that he thought recovery would be an issue. It seemed he'd been at least semi-erect from the moment they'd met. But he wanted to be inside her the first time he came. With that in mind, he dug his wallet out of his jeans and retrieved the condom.

Audrey snatched it from his hands and ripped it open.

"You first," he said.

"I've already been twice today, and I've pretty much been wet ever since. We go together this time." To end the discussion, she sheathed him.

He lifted her up onto an empty counter, stepping between her thighs and pulling her to the edge. Skimming his hands from her knees to her hips, he searched for some control. This wasn't how he'd imagined their first time. It had been a very long time for her. He'd wanted to give her some romance, some tenderness.

But Audrey wrapped her fingers around his cock, positioning him at her entrance and lifting her mouth to his. "Now. Please, Hudson, I need you inside me now."

He slipped slowly inside her. She was tight, her inner muscles already beginning to ripple around him as he retreated and pressed in again, then again, achingly slow, until he was buried in all that wet heat. Nothing had ever felt more perfect than the grip of her body around him. He held still as she adjusted to him, dragging his focus to her face. Her eyes were closed, her breath held.

Taking a hard grip on his own desire, Hudson lifted a hand to her cheek. "Audrey? You okay?"

Those eyes opened and the blue was almost swallowed by her pupils. "You feel so good," she moaned, hands digging into his shoulders. "More."

As relief surged through him, he took her mouth and began to move. She gave as good as she got, rocking against him until his control hung by a thread.

"Deeper." To emphasize the order, she wrapped her legs around his waist and squeezed.

Surrounded by her body, her scent, her vitality, Hudson lost it. Gripping her hips, he pounded into her, grinding against her clit with every thrust, chasing her fire with fevered intensity, until they were both gasping, groaning, lost to the pleasure. Her head dropped to his shoulder and she bit down to hold in the scream as she broke apart in his arms. The feel of her teeth, the clench of her body, ripped away the last of his control. It dragged him over the edge, until he poured out his own shuddering release.

They stayed that way, still joined, for long minutes, as ragged breathing eased. He came back to himself, registering the feel of her sweat dampened skin stuck to his, the perfect weight of her in his arms. He felt alive for the first time in ages. On the heels of that realization came the barest edge of guilt. He was alive.

At last, Audrey lifted her head and brushed her lips over his. "Oh yeah, we have to find a bed."

Hudson huffed out a laugh with what breath he had left. Which was amazing. She was amazing. And he intended to enjoy that for however much time they had left.

11

"SOOOOO, YOU GOT IN awfully late last night." Sam's sing-song voice greeted Audrey as she came out of the bathroom, wrapped in a towel.

"So I did," she confirmed, moving across to pull fresh underwear out of her bag.

"And?"

"And what?" Audrey asked, keeping her expression bland. "I was with Hudson."

"Yeah, but were you *with* him?"

Courtesy of the extra backup condom in his wallet, they'd spent quite a while longer exhausting each other before finally stumbling back to their cabins a few hours before dawn. At the memory, a blush heated Audrey's cheeks.

Sam squealed and knelt on her bed, clutching a pillow in her arms. "Oh my God, tell me everything!"

"That's personal."

"Oh, come on! Girl code! Those who are getting lucky must share the delicious details with those who are regrettably single."

"No sparks between you and Charlie?"

"Please. He's like my delightfully playful brother. Actually, my brother's a Navy SEAL, so he's a helluva lot *more* playful. If I wanted to short sheet somebody or make an underwear raid in the middle of the night, Charlie's my man. But he's not a candidate for warming my bed. For now, I must live vicariously through you. Is what's underneath the clothes as impressive as what I imagine?"

Shimmying into a pair of light cargo pants, Audrey gave in. This was one of those female rituals she'd always envied from the outside. How often did she have anything worth sharing? "It's better. His job does amazing things for that body. As to the rest...God was generous with the good genes."

Sam muffled an envious scream in her pillow. "I'm not going to ask if he was good. You're glowing."

Audrey felt amazing. She hadn't even cared that her PT took extra time or that she was feeling sore muscles in places she'd forgotten she had. After they met for a late breakfast, she and Hudson would be putting their heads together to figure out exactly where they could find some privacy to work them out even more. Her vote was for somewhere they could be clothing optional the rest of the week. It seemed a shame to cover up any of that magnificent body of his. She wondered how long a box of condoms would last.

"You two seem to have gotten pretty close since we've been here. Are y'all gonna keep in touch after camp?"

And just like that, her erotic fantasy collapsed. She tugged on a shirt and didn't meet Sam's gaze. "We're adhering to a strict, no talking about the end of camp policy."

"But—"

A brisk knock on the cabin door cut her off.

Not caring who was on the other side, Audrey called out, "Come in."

The door opened and Hudson all but bounded through, the grin on his face almost as bright as the sun slanting through the windows. He crossed the room in two strides and scooped Audrey off her feet, spinning her in a circle and kissing her senseless in a matter of seconds.

When he collapsed back on her bed, cushioning their fall, she gasped out, "Well, good morning to you, too!"

"John moved his hand. Rachel was talking to him yesterday, asking him questions, and he squeezed hers back." The eyes that had been stormy and gray seemed lighter as he smiled up at her.

"That's wonderful!" Audrey didn't know a whole lot about traumatic brain injuries or comas, but she hoped that this was only the first in a long line of victories for his friend. And she hoped it merited the explosion of hope it had inspired in Hudson.

"We're going to celebrate," he announced.

"Well okay then!"

"How do you feel about camping?" He laced his hands behind her back, keeping her sprawled out over the top of him.

As Audrey couldn't find reason to complain about the position, she relaxed. "Like in a tent, packing in all our gear, away from civilization kind of camping?"

"Like shared sleeping bag and all the s'mores you can eat away from civilization kind of camping."

Alone time. Hell yes. "I'm game."

"How fast can you be ready?"

It turned out Audrey could get ready a lot faster than they could gather up the requisite gear from camp. But after lunch they set out with loaded packs and a map of the surrounding area. Camp Firefly Falls had a section set aside for primitive camping, but it wasn't secluded enough for their purposes, so Hudson had arranged for a permit to camp in the national park on the other side of the lake. The hike in took about three hours, as they stopped for frequent breaks. Audrey knew that was for her benefit and appreciated that he didn't seem to resent it. Hudson himself seemed so hyped up, he could've run a marathon, pack and all. By the time he'd decided on a campsite—a lovely copse of trees about fifteen yards from a stream—she was more than ready to get things set up and start dinner.

At his direction, she began assembling the tent poles.

"John, Steve, and I used to do this all the time growing up."

It was the first time he'd mentioned his friends without a shadow of pain. "Yeah? You all grew up in Syracuse, right?"

"Within half a mile of each other. We started out with pup tents in the back yard. Graduated on up to a tree house when we were ten. Then Boy Scouts."

He continued to talk as they put up the tent, telling stories about their adventures. Every word built a picture of rock solid, life-long friendship that was as foreign to Audrey as the dark side of the moon. She wanted that. Ached for it somewhere down deep. It was far too late for her, but she wanted that for her children someday. Children she could suddenly picture with clear gray eyes.

"—but really, all we needed was a sleeping bag, pocket knife, flashlight, water, and peanut butter sandwiches."

Audrey swallowed against a throat gone dry and forced a smile. "I hope we have something with a bit more substance for dinner."

"S'mores, of course. I haven't looked to see what else they packed, but the kitchen staff assured me it was a rustic, romantic dinner for two."

"Romantic, huh?"

He offered a faux casual shrug as he threaded the pole through the loops on the nylon tent. "I might've let slip I wanted to impress a girl."

"You impress me daily."

"I'm about to impress you more. I brought a surprise."

"Oh yeah?" Interested, she watched as he wrestled something out of the bottom of his pack.

"I made a run into town. That's part of why it took so long."

Audrey angled her head to read the side of the box. "You bought us an air mattress?"

"I figured we had plans." He waggled his eyebrows. "Besides, it's not good for you to sleep on the hard ground. I want you to enjoy this trip and be as comfortable as possible. Even if I risk being accused of glamping."

Audrey's heart gave a painful squeeze. He'd gone out of his way—again—to make sure she was taken care of. She knew he didn't think of himself as a hero, and yet he kept proving that he was, day after day, with the big things and the small. He made her feel valued and cherished in a way no one ever had. How could she ever walk away from this man? The hero of her heart.

Because she didn't want to make a big thing out of it, she injected a lightness to her tone as she slid her arms around his shoulder. "I appreciate your willingness to risk your man card on my behalf and will be happy to reward you appropriately later on."

"I definitely like the sound of that. Especially

since I haven't even shown you the best feature of this thing."

"What's that?" she asked.

Hudson's lips curved in a wicked grin. "It's self-inflating."

"Thoughtful *and* expedient. I do love a man who can plan." And as he set about unrolling the air mattress and flipping on the blower, Audrey was forced to admit—to herself, at least—that she'd fallen in love with this one.

"IF WE DON'T UNZIP the door, do you suppose we can pretend it isn't morning?" As Audrey's bare shoulder was only a couple of inches from his mouth, Hudson pressed a kiss there.

With a sleepy, satisfied purr, she stretched back against him, then winced.

He propped up on an elbow and looked down at her, worried he'd overdone it. "You okay?"

She grimaced. "I'm afraid I do a very good impersonation of an arthritic octogenarian first thing in the morning. It takes a lot of stretching and PT exercises to get me moving."

"Let me help."

Hudson took it as progress when she only

smiled. "First time I've done them naked, with company."

He knew they'd have to pack up and head back to camp soon, but he wasn't in any hurry to leave their private little oasis. And Hudson, Jr. was ever hopeful of one last repeat performance. "I'm a firm believer in positive reinforcement for completing your mandatory PT."

Her eyes sparkled. "I have been known to reward myself with chocolate for breakfast. But we finished that off last night with the s'mores."

"I expect we can come up with a suitable replacement."

A feline smile curved her lips as her gaze dropped to his crotch, where his cock was already stirring again. "Mmm, yes please."

"So polite." Hudson took the leg she offered and followed her instructions for where and how to stretch it. Before releasing it, he dug his fingers into the muscles, massaging the stiffness. Audrey made a sound very close to the moans of pleasure he'd coaxed out of her when they'd made love at dawn.

He'd miss this. He'd miss her. And that had his brain treading perilously close to that whole topic of life outside of camp that they were avoiding. But maybe...maybe they didn't have to. "Why were you in Syracuse?"

Her lashes fluttered back open. "What?"

"Two years ago. Why were you in Syracuse?"

Those blue eyes went sharp on his. "I was driving cross country from Toronto to Yale for a seminar."

"Yale?"

"Mmm. It's where I went to graduate school."

Over the past days, it had been easy to forget she was a girl genius. She didn't talk about work. But Ivy League grad school at *nineteen*. Damn. "What exactly does one do with a Ph.D. in sociology from Yale?"

"Research usually. It's what I was doing before the accident. I wound up in Chattanooga because they offered me a teaching position that I could still manage around my surgeries and physical therapy. Most of my classes are online. But I'm healed up, so it's time for me to rejoin the real world professionally."

"And you'll have to leave Chattanooga to do that?" Hudson kept his voice casual.

"Yeah. The next logical step is taking a tenure track position at a large research university." She paused, beginning to work the other leg. "I interviewed for a position at UC Berkeley right before I came to camp."

"California." It might as well be Australia.

She sighed with an utter lack of enthusiasm that had an unreasonable surge of hope burgeoning in his chest. "Yeah. If they offered me the job, it would be a big feather in my professional cap, get me back on the fast track, almost as if the accident never happened."

"But?" *Please let there be a but.*

"I don't actually like California. They don't have real seasons out there. Not like I'm used to. And..."

Hudson's heart began to pound as he waited for her to continue. When she didn't, he prompted, "And?"

"And—this is practically heresy in my family—I don't know if I still want the things I wanted before the accident. With everything my parents sacrificed for my education, I'm pretty sure they'd have a cow if I walked away from all that. But I've gotten to where I like the slower pace. I'd never have had the time for something like Camp Firefly Falls in a research position. It's all about publish or perish, eighty-hour work weeks, and always pursuing the next grant. I...can't imagine going back to that." She gave a little laugh. "Which is a moot point. They haven't offered me the job, and considering I've been out of mainstream academia for two years, they probably won't."

It sounded like a misery to him. He began to massage her other calf. "What *do* you want?"

She was silent so long, he didn't think she'd answer. "Marriage. Family. A *life.* When I'm ninety, I don't want to be in a place where I've got academic accolades out the wazoo but no one to sit by a fire and read with. If I were in a different discipline and my research held the potential to be life changing, maybe I'd feel differently. But that's not what I do. What I've done. Not that I couldn't change my area of research to something more impactful, but...figuring out the why of things just doesn't seem as important as it used to. And I haven't figured out what to do with that. It's a scary thing finding out that the path you've been certain of your whole life isn't necessarily the right one."

"Did you really pick that path or did your parents kinda shove you on it?"

She considered the question. "Hard to say at this point. I was on board from the beginning. I'd still be on board if not for the accident. I guess, in a way, I'm grateful it happened."

"Really?"

She tugged her leg free and sat up, brushing a

quick kiss over his lips. "It brought me you." Her hand slid into the hair at his nape. "However long it lasts, I'm beyond grateful for that."

Emotion tangled in his chest—a bittersweet mix of regret for the brevity of their time and a longing for something he hardly dared hope could be a possibility. She was a gift. A reminder that not all the world was darkness and despair. Hudson laced his hand with hers and brought them to his lips. "I'm grateful for you." For more things than he was prepared to say. So, he laid her back and showed her instead.

Much later, they strolled back into Camp Firefly Falls holding hands like a couple of giddy teenagers.

"Not gonna lie. I'm going to hog every drop of hot water in the shower," Audrey declared.

He hooked an arm around her shoulders as they went up her cabin steps. "You could share. Really, it's the environmentally responsible thing to do."

"You cannot possibly—Can you?"

Hudson shrugged. It seemed worth the ache in his balls to try for the chance to see her naked, wet, and soapy. "Looks like Sam's out. We could hang a sock on the door."

"You're incorrigible." But she grinned as she said it.

The phone in his pocket buzzed as several texts hit at once.

Audrey dumped her pack. "You get that. I'll go start the shower and let the water warm up."

Admiring her very fine backside, Hudson fished out his phone to find two missed calls and several text messages from Rachel. They all had the same theme, with an increasing level of urgency. *Call me.*

He dialed immediately. She picked up on the second ring.

"Rach? I've been out of cell range. What's up?"

"Hud, I..." At the strain in her voice, his hand tightened on the phone.

"Rachel?"

"John's gone, Hud."

The denial was swift and automatic. "No. No. You said he was getting better. He squeezed your hand."

Audrey came out of the bathroom, her hand covering her mouth.

On the phone, Rachel was still talking, her tone choked. "The doctors warned us this was a possibility in the beginning. A probability."

"No," Hudson snarled. "There are things they

could have done, kept him going until he could get better."

"Hudson." Rachel's voice was gentle. "You know how he felt about life support. He didn't want to be hooked up to machines, and he filed a do not resuscitate order."

In some dim, distant part of his brain, Hudson recognized that he was out of line. That taking his grief out on John's widow was beyond a dick thing to do. But that realization was drowned out by the grief that battered him like hail.

John was dead.

Yesterday, he'd been alive. He'd been alive and responsive for the first time in three months. And instead of getting in his Jeep and driving home, Hudson had taken that news as a sign from God that he could let go and live again himself. That his friend was on the mend. That they'd have more time. He'd missed Rachel's messages. And he'd missed his chance to say goodbye.

12

AUDREY'S HEART CRACKED RIGHT in two as Hudson stood there, broad shoulders rigid, hand white knuckling the phone. It was obvious that his celebration yesterday had been premature, and the worst had come to pass. Tears clogged her own throat on his behalf. This would break him in a way nothing else could.

"Did he ever wake up?" The voice that had been full of fun and laughter just minutes before now trembled.

His shoulders slumped at Rachel's answer. For a few more minutes, he listened, grunting monosyllabic responses as a muscle jumped in his jaw. "I'll be there."

As soon as he hung up the phone, Audrey crossed the room. She wasn't even sure he saw her. But she slid her arms around him anyway, needing to do anything she could to comfort him. "I'm so sorry."

He stood rigid, his breath ragged. She held him tighter, willing him to take what she offered. At long last, he wrapped around her, burying his face in her hair. He began to shake, the force of the emotions he was holding back almost too great to bear. Audrey wanted to tell him to just let go, that he didn't have to be strong with her, that he could grieve. But she didn't know how he'd respond. Instead she stroked his back, hoping the fact that he wasn't alone was, at least, a little bit of comfort.

"I'm going home." His voice was muffled, thick with emotion.

"Of course, you are." He'd hardly stay at camp after this. The funeral would probably be in a few days. "When?"

He pulled away. "Today. Now."

Even expecting it, Audrey couldn't stop the visceral rejection of that. No. She'd just found him. She wasn't ready to let him go. But she swallowed back the protests. This wasn't about her. "Okay. I'll help you pack."

Recognizing that he needed to move, she towed him toward the door. Hudson dropped her hand to scoop up his pack and followed. They didn't speak on the walk to his cabin. Nor did they touch. With every step, she could feel him retreating from her, and she didn't know what to do about it.

Charlie wasn't at the cabin, and she was grateful to have a little while longer alone with Hudson. They went through the motions, gathering up his stuff. When he would have just shoved it all into his bags, she stopped to fold things, wanting to delay his departure and not at all sure he was in any shape to drive. She didn't dare ask if he was okay. He clearly wasn't.

"Maybe you should wait a little bit, until you've had some time to process this, before you get behind the wheel."

The gaze he turned on her was flat, a desolate nothing that was worse than anger or pain. "They're waiting for me. I need to go."

He needed to run. To escape. Desperation was clear in every staccato movement. He was barely holding it together, and Audrey was terrified of what might happen when he really broke.

"I could come with you." The words were out

before she could think better of them. It was too soon, too intimate. A thing you offered when you were in a true relationship, and they were...Audrey didn't know what they were. But they'd shared more than just fun and laughter this week. More than sex. That had to count for something.

"What?"

"I could go back to Syracuse with you."

"Why?"

His tone was so baffled, she regretted making the offer. But she'd already started down this path, so she pushed on. "For you. To be a support. To help. Whatever you need."

For the first time since they'd met, Hudson stared at her like the freak she'd so often felt like. The strange one. The out-of-sync. And she knew she'd said the wrong thing.

"This is my real life, Audrey. The real world. Whatever we've had, whatever this has been, ends at the camp property line. We agreed on that."

No, they'd agreed not to talk about it. Maybe an ending had been implicit, but she'd thought, after last night—

"There's no room for this where I'm going. You're a distraction I can't afford."

He was grieving, angry at the world and blaming himself. She was the nearest target. But even seeing that, knowing it, didn't diminish the pain of his words. How could he reduce what they'd shared to a mere distraction?

Audrey knit her hands and hated herself for the show of weakness. She had to work at keeping her voice steady. "You've helped me through so much. I just wanted to return the favor."

"I appreciate the thought, but I don't need help."

"Everybody needs help sometimes. There's no shame in that."

"And what help would you be, exactly? You need rescuing every time you turn around. I can't be that guy. Especially not now. I've got too much on my plate."

She flinched away as if he'd struck her. "I didn't ask you to rescue me," she whispered. "I didn't ask for any of this."

"Neither did I." He tossed his duffel bags over his shoulder. "Goodbye, Audrey." And without another word, he walked out.

She sank down on his bed, her knees knocking together too hard to continue to stand. She was still sitting there some time later when Charlie and Sam came into the cabin, laughing and joking.

"Audrey! You're back! How did the great camping trip go?" Sam asked.

"Hey, where's Hudson's stuff?" Charlie asked.

Audrey raised her head to look at them, her whole body feeling leaden from her own grief. "Gone," she managed and burst into tears.

"Firefighter John Matthew McCleary— Lehigh County Dispatch."

The sound of the radio was too loud over the sober masses by the graveside. It raked Hudson's already raw nerves and made him want to scream. The waiting silence as the dispatcher began John's last call was worse.

"Firefighter John Matthew McCleary—Lehigh County Dispatch."

Hud's hands curled to fists as he stared at the flag-draped coffin on the little dais beneath the tent. He wanted to think his heart couldn't break any further, but every moment of this funeral shattered it just a little more.

"Having heard no response, we know that Firefighter McCleary has responded to his last call on Earth and that the fire department in the hereafter has a new responder."

A soft, choked noise came from Rachel as the dispatcher continued.

"Firefighter McCleary served the citizens of Lehigh County for twelve years. We appreciate Firefighter McCleary's dedication and his family's sacrifices during the time he was a Firefighter. Your warm laugh and ready smile will be missed." The dispatcher's voice hitched for a moment before she continued. "Firefighter McCleary, you have now become a Guardian who will help watch out for all Firefighters as they respond to emergencies. You've completed your tour as a Firefighter in this life and are clear to remain with the Lord forever. Goodbye, and we'll take it from here."

The dispatcher signed off, advising all units of a moment of silence.

When it was done, the bugler, set up on a hill about twenty-five yards away, began to play TAPS. Hudson stepped toward the casket, along with another of the honor guard, and began to fold the flag. It was a ritual he'd performed just months ago for Steve. He'd barely held it together for Steve's mom. The fresh pain of John's death all but took him to his knees as his hands performed their duty. He clenched his teeth, forcing himself to hold on to his emotions for Rachel's sake. Per ceremony, he turned to present the flag to the fire chief, who turned and knelt, presenting it to Rachel. John's widow, who would never again hear her husband laugh or make jokes, would never bear his children, or grow old by his side. In unrelieved black and the pearls John had given her for their fifth anniversary, she clutched the flag, lifting her eyes to Hudson's.

God, how could she even look at him?

Shame that he was the reason for this clogged his throat. But he didn't look away. He owed Rachel that much. They held each other's gaze, lost in shared grief, until Hudson realized the other mourners were filing away. The funeral was over. Everything was over. And he didn't have the first clue how to go on living. He moved to Rachel, wanting to offer—what? His condolences? His service? His life? The wish that he could trade places with John and give them the long life together they'd deserved? Nothing would ever be enough to make up for John's sacrifice.

"Rach, I—" What could he say? In the end, he said nothing, wrapping his arms around her. As she rested her head against his chest, the flag trapped between them, he looked away, searching the crowds for some kind of an answer, some sort of guidance.

A flash of red hair had him going stock still, his heart shooting into his throat. But the woman walking away from the graveside had too even a gait in the three-inch heels and none of the scars crisscrossing the legs that were bare beneath the black funeral dress. Not Audrey. Of course, it wouldn't be Audrey. He'd made it perfectly, painfully clear where they stood that last day at camp. Nowhere.

It had to be that way. When she'd made her offer, every cell in his body had wanted to grab her up and fall to his knees in thanks that she was willing to endure this with him. And he didn't deserve that kindness. He didn't deserve any sort of a buffer against the grief and guilt. How could he possibly have accepted her offer of support, when Rachel was here with no one? Never mind the friends and family who'd turned out, lining the streets of town. She was alone because of him, and Hudson couldn't even think of moving on with his own life now.

So, he'd lashed out, striking at her in the only way that would ensure she'd stay at camp and not do something crazy like come up to Syracuse on her own. In his way, he'd meant it. There was no room for her in the life he had here. Because eventually her sweet nature and enthusiasm for the second chance she'd been given would heal him—which he didn't deserve. Or those same things he loved about her would dim. Her light would go out in the face of the toxic shit that was his world right now—and she deserved better than that. So, he'd been cruel, saving her one last time, this time from him.

No, Audrey wouldn't be coming back into his life. But he realized, as he stared at the retreating back of the other woman, that a part of him had been looking for her anyway.

"Hud? What is it?" Rachel was following his gaze.

He shook himself. "It's nothing."

She'd be expected back at the house for the reception. It would be overflowing with family, friends, other first responders. He dreaded the whole thing and couldn't imagine how she was bearing up so well under the strain. But he'd be there. He'd do whatever could be done to lighten her load. He'd take care of her in John's absence.

With a sigh, he steeled himself. "Are you ready?" The moment the words were out, he wished he could take them back. Was anyone ever ready to face the endless sympathy and parade of casseroles that hammered home the death of a loved one?

Rachel kissed her fingers, then laid them over the polished wood of the coffin. The finality of the gesture gutted him. Then she straightened her shoulders and took the arm he offered. "Let's go honor my husband."

13

"THEY'RE SETTING UP FOR the talent show in the lodge. You should come." Sam's voice was overly cheerful, as if by sheer will alone she could counter Audrey's melancholy.

Audrey glanced up at her from her potter's wheel and didn't move, her hands still wrapped around the rhythmic turning of the clay. "I'm fine here."

"Honey, you've been holed up in here for days. We're going home day after tomorrow. I don't want to see you skipping out on the last of camp."

Audrey would've happily gone home as soon as Hudson left. If Sam hadn't been with her, she would have. But they'd paid for the full two weeks and Sam was having a blast, so she'd stayed. Everything at Camp Firefly Falls reminded her of Hudson and made her ache—being here in the pottery studio especially. But she'd found it soothing before him, and she'd be damned if he'd ruin that for her, too. So, she'd stayed hidden, avoiding the other campers, and counting down the days until she could leave.

"I'm itching to get back to work." Which was a partial truth. She was itching to get back to the university, to a world that made sense to her, where she knew the expectations.

Sam knit her hands, her brow furrowed with distress. "Audrey."

"I'm fine."

"You're not. You're barely eating. You're not sleeping. I'm worried about you."

Audrey sighed. She'd appreciate the friendship later, but right now, she just wanted to be alone in her misery. "Okay, I'm not. But I'll *be* fine when we get home." Where she wouldn't think of Hudson everywhere she turned.

"I'm sorry I pushed you into pursuing him."

"You didn't push me into anything I wasn't gunning for myself. And you hardly pushed me into bed with him. I made that decision on my own." Because it hadn't been simple attraction pulling them together. They'd found something with each other. Something she'd come to treasure. She just...hadn't expected he'd let it go so easily.

"Are you in love with him?" Sam asked quietly.

Audrey dropped her head, wishing her hair was loose instead of gathered in a knot at her nape, so she could hide from the question. Because she'd known the answer when they'd gone camping, and she didn't want to think about the truth of it.

"I think...I've been a little bit in love with a fantasy version of him since he pulled me out of that car. But the time with him here? Getting to know the real man? That just blew the fantasy out of the water."

Sam laid a hand on Audrey's shoulder. "I'm so sorry he hurt you."

"He didn't do it deliberately." Audrey was rational enough to recognize that. He was drowning in grief and guilt and shoving her away because he didn't believe he deserved anything good in his life. Not that what he'd said stung any less. "And he never made me any promises. I was the one who tried to change the rules." Because she cared about him, and she was worried about how he was coping with John's death. She was still worried.

Not that she'd heard from him. He was well and truly out of her life. It was on her to learn how to live with that.

The outside door to the building opened. Audrey hoped someone else was coming to work in the studio and that it would put a stop to Sam's well-intentioned attempts to talk about this.

Heather stepped into the room. "Hey Audrey. I was hoping I'd find you here. You've got a phone call up at the lodge."

Audrey's fingers flexed, and the wall of her vase dipped in, the whole thing collapsing. "Who is it?"

"I don't know, but he was very insistent that he talk to you. He's still on hold."

Hudson. A surge of hope had her fumbling to turn off the wheel. She dumped the entire failed vase into the scrap bucket, quickly washing her hands. "Lead the way."

Was the funeral over? Had he realized he needed her? Did he regret what he'd said? Maybe he just wanted to apologize. The possibilities rolled around in her head like a bag of spilled marbles, shooting off in all directions. By the time they made it to the lodge office, her heart was tripping double time.

"I'll just give you some privacy." Heather shut the door behind her.

Audrey scooped up the receiver. "Hello, this is Audrey."

"Dr. Graham! This is Dr. Feinstein out at UC Berkeley."

Surprise was quickly chased by disappointment. Of course, it wouldn't be Hudson. Why should anything have changed with him? He'd made his position perfectly clear.

She struggled to keep her tone professional. "Sir. How unexpected to hear from you."

"Yes, I apologize for bothering you on your vacation. I got the number from your parents. It's just that the board has made a decision, and I didn't want to wait to get in touch with you. We're delighted to offer you a position on our faculty."

Shock stole her voice for a long moment. She hadn't even thought about Berkeley since she got to camp, other than briefly mentioning the interview to Hudson, and here the department head was offering Audrey her textbook perfect job on a platter.

Her brain kicked in. *Say something.* "I...wow. I'm so flattered." She ought to be beyond flattered. This was what she'd been waiting for, a chance to get back to the academic fast track and make up for lost time. No one could have predicted that they'd jump at her with the two-year gap in research.

"I'm sure you're entertaining multiple offers, and we wanted to get in at the front of the pack."

She listened as Dr. Feinstein continued to talk about the details of the offer, making notes and asking questions, re-engaging the academic side of her brain. And it was good to feel wanted, mollifying to feel respected. This was her world. The place where she was most comfortable. As the conversation continued, she found herself getting excited about academia again. The position would be a challenge. She hadn't had a real mental challenge, something she could sink her teeth into, since before the accident.

Well, she'd had Hudson. She'd felt...needed and useful trying to help him embrace life again. But she'd failed him in the end. He wouldn't take his second chance at life. But maybe she could explore that area in formal research. It was something to consider.

"I still need some time to think about it before I give a final answer."

"Of course. Of course." Dr. Feinstein was all agreeableness. "We look forward to hearing from you and hope you'll be joining our faculty this fall."

As Audrey told him goodbye and hung up, she considered that maybe this was exactly the sign she'd been waiting for.

~

HUDSON SHUT the door to Rachel's house after the last guest. "I'm glad that's over."

From her position on the sofa, Rachel kicked off her pumps and flexed her feet. "It was good, though. To hear all the stories."

"John was well loved." Hudson crossed back to the living room, slipping off his dress uniform coat and draping it over a chair. "Want a drink?"

"God, yes. There's wine in the kitchen."

He poured her a glass, then cracked open the fridge to grab a beer. But there wasn't one. Because Rachel didn't drink beer, and John hadn't lived here in three months. Wishing for something stronger now, he splashed some more of the wine into a second glass for himself and went back to join Rachel on the sofa.

"I'm glad everybody shared their pictures." She took the wine and continued to scroll through image after image on her laptop. John at picnics or family functions. John around town. Some were of John at work, cleaning or storing equipment or otherwise horsing around the firehouse. Steve was in so many, and so was Hudson. They'd both been an inextricable part of his life, and without them, it felt like everything was unraveling.

"Have you added yours?" she asked.

"Not sure what all I've got." Hudson pulled out his phone and unlocked it before handing it over to Rachel. He took a testing sip of the wine. Not his preference, but it didn't totally suck.

Rachel had paused on some picture or other, an odd expression on her face.

"What is it?" he asked. Man, had one of the guys taken some kind of compromising picture he didn't know about? Maybe he should've pre-screened what was on there.

She turned the phone around. "Who is she?"

From the screen a familiar, smiling face stared out, pressed cheek-to-cheek with his. Hud felt a stab of pain at the sight of it. "Audrey."

Rachel rolled her eyes. "Which tells me next to nothing. Who is she *to you?* A woman you met at camp?"

He took a bigger gulp of wine. "Not exactly. I worked an accident she was in a couple years ago." He told her about the wreck and how Audrey had ended up at Camp Firefly Falls.

"Wow. That seems like kismet."

Of course, Rachel, with her gooshy, romantic heart, would think that. "It's just a small world."

"You spent a lot of time with her?"

Only every waking minute. "A fair bit."

"You're smiling in this picture."

Hud knew she was fishing. Under other circumstances he'd have shut this line of questioning down fast. But this was as much about distraction for her as interest in what had been going on with him. "Yeah. It was a good day." She'd made him take basket weaving with her. The corner of his mouth quirked as he remembered her excitement.

"I never thought I'd see that."

He drained the wine and shrugged. "Haven't had a lot of cause for smiling since the accident."

"It's not even that. I've known you since we were in diapers, and I've *never* seen you smile like this, Hud."

There was no good answer to that.

She laid a hand on his arm. "I'm sorry the timing worked out like this and we had to call you home."

Covering her hand with his was automatic. "It's fine." It was probably for the best. He'd gotten in over his head. Another few days with her and he might've started considering something drastic, and that was just crazy. His family, his duty, were here.

"When are you going to see her again?"

There went that pang again. He'd give almost anything for another chance to hold her, to hear her laugh. But that wasn't gonna happen. He'd made sure of that. "I'm not."

"What do you mean you're not?"

"I mean today's the last day of camp. Everybody goes home tomorrow. She lives in Tennessee." Or she'd be moving to California or Timbuktu. Somewhere that was far, far away from him. And after how he'd treated her, Hudson couldn't blame her.

"So? There's this thing called a phone and modern transportation."

"Chattanooga isn't exactly a hop, skip, and a jump, Rach. And I don't have any of her contact information. Besides all that, she's not going to want to see me again."

"Why not? It looks like she adores you. And that the feeling is mutual."

"We didn't exactly part on great terms."

Rachel frowned. "Did she have some problem with you leaving early?"

"She offered to come with me." How many times in the past few days had he wished he'd taken her up on that offer? How many times had he wanted to reach for her, to feel her arms around him in that calm, quiet way she had?

"Why didn't she?"

Hudson didn't want to talk about this anymore. He started to rise, but Rachel tightened her grip on his arm.

"Why didn't she come, Hud?"

"Because I shot her down." Even as he'd done it, he'd felt like such an asshole.

"Why?"

"Because you don't bring a woman you've known less than two weeks to your best friend's funeral. And you sure as hell don't flaunt her in front of his widow." He shoved up and began to pace. "I had to shut things down. Things were getting too serious, and I can't do serious." Even if he could, he'd destroyed her trust in him, left her bleeding.

Rachel stared at him, mouth agape. "What the hell is wrong with you?"

"Excuse me?"

"You can't do serious? Hudson, you're one of the most committed people I know."

"It doesn't change anything. My commitment has to be here. To you, to the family, to my company."

"This isn't about me or your family or the company. The only thing you're committed to is acting like you never got pulled out of that fire."

Hudson stopped dead. "Excuse me?"

"I get that you're grieving. That's natural and proper. But John did not haul your ass out of that burning building so that you could curl up and pretend you died anyway. He hauled you out because he loved you. So you would live. This whole retreat from the world and everything good in it routine you've had going since the fire is an insult to John and a disservice to everything he stood for. He gave you a second chance at life. How dare you do anything but use it?"

"Use it? What? I'm supposed to just go on, every day, like John's death isn't *my fault?*"

"Yes, damn it. Because it wasn't your fault."

"He died because he came after me. I don't know how you can even look at me."

"If he hadn't gone after you, he wouldn't have been the man I loved from the time I was fourteen. He believed in the job, and I believed in him. We knew the risks. And yes, I lost the love of my life. But I don't blame you for it. You need to stop blaming yourself."

Hudson didn't know what that looked like and couldn't understand how she could even think it.

"How can you be so calm about this? We just put your husband in the ground this morning."

"Because I lost him three months ago. I knew it. The doctors knew it. Everyone knew it but you. You were the only one who expected he'd wake up."

"You just gave up?"

"No. I hoped and prayed every day. But he couldn't come back from that, and it was time for him to let go." She came to him, wrapping her arms around him in a tight hug. "Now it's your turn. You have to let go of this half-life, Hud. You have to honor him by living."

He buried his face in her hair, barely able to speak past the pain in his chest. "I don't know how."

Rachel pulled back to look into his face. "I think you know someone who can teach you."

Wasn't that what Audrey had been doing the entire time at camp? Encouraging him to embrace life again? He'd done it for her. Now it was time to do it for himself.

Even as he thought it, he remembered the look of devastation on her face. All that time spent protecting her from every imagined danger, and he'd deliberately, callously, hit her where he knew it would hurt the most. The back of Hudson's neck got hot. "I was an asshole when I left."

"So, get your ass on the road and go apologize. You have one more night to make it right. Go make the most of it."

Hudson didn't know if he could make it right. He didn't know if she'd ever want to see him again. But he had to go and try to repair the damage he'd done to her and set the record straight.

14

"IT IS THE LAST night of camp. You are not spending it holed up in our cabin or the pottery studio." Hands on hips, Sam glared at Audrey. "So, get dressed. Or don't. I don't actually care. But you're going to that dance tonight if I have to get Charlie to toss you over his shoulder."

Audrey just arched a brow. "You'd really haul me to the boathouse in my bathrobe?"

"In a New York minute."

Audrey knew she was just crazy enough to do it.

Sam flopped down on the bed. "Honey, I know this whole trip didn't turn out like you wanted, but you can't let your last memory of camp be of moping around."

Audrey wanted to protest that she hadn't been moping, but it would've been a lie. The truth was, all hurt aside, she missed Hudson. And she was worried about how he was coping with his friend's death. Which was wasted emotion. He wasn't a part of her life. Not in any permanent way. That was something she'd come to understand about camp flings—they were intense and glorious because of their brevity.

Would things have been the same between them if there'd been no expiration date? If they'd just met again under circumstances where they could've taken their time, would their attraction still have happened? Or was it just the enforced proximity here at camp that had pulled him into her orbit? Given the hard-core case of survivor's guilt he had going, she might have had the chance to give her thanks, but that would've been it. And she'd have been the poorer for it.

"Please come tonight. At least for a little while."

Audrey didn't want to go. Being around all those happy people, all that noise and boisterous enthusiasm made her want to burrow under the covers and sleep until morning, when they'd be boarding the bus to head back to New York and the airport. But given her luck, their companions on the bus would quiz her about who she was and why she'd been a hermit during camp. Or, worse, ask her what happened with the hottie firefighter who'd saved her ass from death by campfire that first week. Besides, she knew she'd dampened Sam's own pleasure in the whole camp experience, and that really wasn't fair. She'd used up her quota of lousy friend passes.

"Okay. But if I'm going, then it's not going to be in my bathrobe."

Sam grinned and gave a victory fist pump. "Damn straight. If you're going, you might as well knock some socks off. Please let me do your hair and makeup."

Audrey arched a brow. "Are you about to be channeling your Miss Eden's Ridge pageant days?"

"Hush your mouth. I never did pageants. And anyway, didn't you watch *Miss Congeniality?* They're scholarship programs." Sam rummaged around in her stuff and came up with at least four bottles of hair product and a curling iron.

Audrey held up a hand. "I draw the line at hair tall enough to commune with God."

"Noted. Now go get in the shower."

She took her time, as much to let the hot water beat on her stiff muscles as to procrastinate facing the full contingent of beautification tools at Sam's disposal. By the time she strode out, pleasantly pruney, Sam had a whole station set up. With the panache of a game show host, she waved Audrey to her seat.

"Sit and let me work my magic."

Because it obviously made her friend happy to play stylist, Audrey sat.

"I'm having potentially life-altering thoughts."

Sam's hands paused, roller in hand. "About Hudson?"

"Because of him. About my career, my research."

"I thought you didn't want to do research anymore."

"I didn't know what I wanted to do before. But I'm considering a change in focus. I want to start researching survivor guilt. I couldn't help Hudson with his, but maybe I could discover something in my work that could help others like him."

Sam didn't stop moving. "Can't do that in Chattanooga. So, you've decided to take the job in Berkeley?"

"It's an amazing opportunity. The resources I'd have there are unparalleled. It's got me really excited about getting back to my work." She supposed she owed Hudson for that. It wasn't what she'd wanted from him, but as a consolation prize, at least it was an opportunity to do something with true meaning. She needed that in her life now, more than ever.

"I think it's a good idea. But is Berkeley going to go for it?"

"I'm flying out to discuss it with Dr. Feinstein almost as soon as we get home."

"Well, I wish you luck. Even though I'm going to miss you like crazy."

Audrey reached back to lay a hand on Sam's arm. "I'm going to miss you, too. I'll keep in touch."

"Damn straight. Now be still while I finish this."

Her hair was dried, smoothed, then set in loose waves.

"Hate to tell you, but that's going to fall out within five minutes of me stepping outside. My hair doesn't hold curl."

"With this much product, I could get a two-by-four to curl. Now sit still while I do your makeup."

Like an obedient Barbie, Audrey didn't move while Sam swiped, blended, brushed, accented and slicked. "Am I gonna look like a madam when you're done with me?"

"You're going to look like you, just...more." She finished with one more coat of mascara. "There! Take a look at that."

Audrey was glad she had to go into the bathroom for a mirror. It would give her time to put her poker face on before coming back out. But the face that stared back at her wasn't that of a two-bit movie streetwalker. It was, as Sam had said, just her. Except her eyes were bigger, deeper and her cheekbones popped in a way that gave her face a subtle depth. Her lips were glossed a kissable pink. Not that anybody would be taking advantage of that. Still, she couldn't help but be impressed.

"Wow. You're really good at this."

"I'm Southern. We're trained in proper hair and makeup from the time we're knee-high. Plus, my mama owns a salon. Now come back out and let's pick your outfit."

"There's not a lot to pick *from*. I've been in jeans and cargo pants all week."

"All the more reason to wear this." Sam pulled a dress from her bag. Sleeveless, with a V-neck, it was deep blue, made of that stretchy stuff that never wrinkled. "You would look amazing in this."

She would show her legs in that. The skirt would hit her just below the knees. But Audrey's knee-jerk refusal stalled somewhere on the tip of her tongue as she thought about Hudson's ease with her scars. He'd never made a thing of them, never made her feel like a freak show. They were simply part of her. If he could accept that, maybe she could, too. Besides, the boathouse would be pretty dim lighting.

"Oh, why not?"

By the time Charlie showed up half an hour later, Audrey had managed to unearth a little enthusiasm for the prospect of a dance. Courtesy of Sam's ministrations, she *did* look good—a fact which Charlie underscored with mimed heart palpitations at the sight of her.

"Hubba hubba!"

Audrey laughed. "You are incorrigible."

"What I am is a lucky bastard to have two beautiful ladies to escort tonight." He crooked both his arms. "Shall we?"

Audrey and Sam slid their arms through his.

Audrey stood on her tiptoes and pressed a kiss to his cheek. "Thanks for being a good friend, Charlie."

He covered her hand with his. "Anytime, beautiful. Let's go paint the camp red!"

THE DANCE HAD ALREADY STARTED by the time Hudson rolled back into Camp Firefly Falls. He could hear faint strains of the music thumping as he got out of his Jeep. Would Audrey be there, observing people or would she be off on her own somewhere, away from all the noise? She'd been all about the classic camp experience, and likely everyone was at the boathouse tonight. He trudged in that direction, with no better idea of what he'd say to make things right than he'd had when he left Syracuse two hours before. He'd had plenty of time to replay the scene in his cabin and realize exactly how badly he'd fucked up. He wasn't sure there was an apology big enough to make up for that, but he was sure as hell gonna try.

As it had that first night, the boathouse was jumping. Michael Tully was tending bar again. Though he viciously wanted a beer, Hudson bypassed Michael and wove his way around the edges of the crowd, looking for a familiar flash of red hair. He didn't find her on the first pass. Surely, she hadn't left camp early just because he'd been a dick. God, he hoped he hadn't ruined that for her, too. He started to head to the pottery studio but took one last look out on the dance floor. And there she was, dancing with Charlie and Sam.

She was wearing a dress. And damn, she was a total knockout with her hair and makeup all done up. He knew what it meant for her to show her legs, and for a moment, he was overcome with a fierce pride that she'd done it. It was different to see her all dressed up instead of in the casual camp clothes she'd worn the last couple of weeks —one of the many sides of her he hoped like hell he'd get a chance to see again after tonight.

Locked in on his target, Hudson wove his way through the dancing crowd, rehearsing his apology. He hadn't gotten much past the basic, *I'm sorry* before she caught sight of him. For a fleeting second, she lit up with pleasure, but by the time he made it to her, she'd locked down that reaction. Not a great reception, but the momentary light gave him hope.

"Hi." *Brilliant opening, Lowell.*

For once, Charlie didn't insert himself into the conversation. He just nodded before he and Sam dropped back, presumably to give them some privacy. But the pair of them stayed close.

Audrey crossed her arms over her middle, her posture half-protective, half-defensive. "You came back."

"Yeah. I had to see you."

Over the sound system, Journey rolled into Thomas Rhett's "Die A Happy Man." Appropriate, if she'd forgive him. Hudson held out a hand. "Can I speak to you? Privately."

She hesitated only a second before placing her

hand in his. Sam took a step forward, but Charlie put a restraining hand on her arm. Audrey looked to her friend and gave a tiny shake of her head. Message received. Audrey still trusted him, at least a little. Sam clearly did not.

He wanted to wrap around Audrey, bury his face in her hair, and just hold her until his world righted again. But he'd walked away from the right to do that. So, Hudson led her outside to the pier instead. It seemed appropriate to have this conversation here, where it had all started. She'd been so hesitant that first time he saw her, when she'd followed him outside from the dance—so unsure of her reception. She wasn't hesitant now. Her stride was confident, her back straight. This time he was the one who was uncertain.

Except, no, he realized. That hadn't been the first time he saw her. He'd seen her across the lake that first afternoon. Even from that distance, he'd felt her sense of absolute peace. Envied it. He'd had that with her, for a time, and then he'd destroyed everything.

"I'm sorry." He blurted it out, even knowing he was getting ahead of himself. "I know that doesn't even begin to cover it. I was an asshole, and I hurt you."

"Hudson, I get it. You were grieving."

He didn't deserve the understanding he saw in her face. "Don't make excuses for me. There is no excuse for how I treated you. We both know why I did it, but I have to say it anyway." He had to get this right. Had to fix what he'd broken. "You are the most compassionate person I have ever met. You completely overlooked the fact that I'm a surly, miserable bastard, and did everything you could to pull me out of the pit I'd fallen into. And you did it. You brought me back to life in a very real way. Then John died, and I just lost my shit."

"It's okay. Really, I accept your apology."

"No. No, it's not okay. You offered yourself up to help me, to support me, and I hit at you in the worst possible way. It's not true. You *don't* need rescuing all the time. You've been rescuing yourself perfectly well without me." Hudson could feel himself losing control, hear the edge of it in his voice. Because he realized, standing here, seeing her again, exactly what it was he'd thrown away. He loved this woman, with her gigantic heart and fearless determination.

He wanted to reach for her but didn't dare. Everything in him felt taut as a bowstring, ready to snap in two. He'd lost Steve. He'd lost John. Hudson didn't think he could bear losing Audrey, too.

"The truth is, I'm the one who needed saving. I've been drowning. And I had to push you away because I wanted what you were offering so damned badly that if you didn't back off, I was going to hold on and never let go."

Audrey lost that carefully neutral expression, her eyes glimmering in the moonlight. "Hudson." She stepped into him, wrapping her arms tight around his waist.

Thank God. Thank God.

He drew her against him, feeling something deep inside quiet as her body settled against his. He did wrap around her now, pressing his face to her hair, inhaling her scent, feeling the thud of her heart against his. Right and perfect. It felt like coming home.

As THEY STOOD in the quiet night, the sounds of the party a world away, Audrey held him and stroked his spine. It was impossible not to think about the first time she'd seen him here—embraced him here—so aloof, holding himself back from life, from connection. An island unto himself. Every step of drawing him out had been a journey of discovery. And the real man had been so much more than her fantasies. Before the call about John, he'd been a changed man, still caring and protective, but also fun and alive. Vibrant. This Hudson was something else again. He was hollow and wounded, and it was breaking her heart.

"I'm sorry. I'm so goddamned sorry."

The remorse in his voice was so hard to hear. He hated himself for the things he'd said far more than she ever had—ever could—and that hurt her. God, he was so brittle. But he'd come back to her.

His words played over in her head.

I wanted what you were offering so damned badly that if you didn't back off, I was going to hold on and never let go.

She didn't want him to let go. Relief and elation burned away the misery of the past days, wiped out everything but the need to comfort him. So, Audrey held on and lifted her mouth to his.

He kissed her like a drowning man chasing a last breath of oxygen. His desperation, his fierceness, rocked her. She gave him everything she had, pouring out all the worry, all the tenderness she felt, until the tension slowly leeched out of him.

Breath not altogether steady, Audrey stood, her brow pressed to his. *I love you.* The words beat against her breast, desperate to get out, but she held them back. It was too soon, too…something. She'd pressed too fast before and he'd bolted. Instead, she said, "God, I missed you."

"I missed you, too. More than I ever imagined. I'd have come back sooner but the funeral was today." There was no mistaking the thread of pain underscoring his words.

She wanted to ask how it had gone, but that felt wrong, too. How did any funeral ever go? In any event, he'd survived it and come back to camp. For her. "I've been worried about you."

"The whole time, I kept wishing you were there, wishing I'd said yes." He cupped her face, rubbing a thumb along her cheek. "I wanted to call, but I—I never dreamed you'd forgive me."

"Of course, I forgive you. I'd never hold your grief against you."

Hudson stepped back, running his hands from her shoulders down her arms to take both her hands in his. "I know we said we wouldn't talk about the end of camp. But I need to know you'll give me another chance. A chance for something beyond camp, beyond these two weeks. A chance for something real."

Beyond camp.

Reality came crashing back down on Audrey. Tomorrow it was back to the real world. The real world she'd made plans for without him. Plans that would take her to the other side of the country.

He rolled on, coming as near to babbling as she'd ever heard. "I know it's fast. I know it's crazy. But it was crazy that we found each other in the first place, crazy that we both came here. And I can't just walk away after two weeks. It's not enough."

Her tongue wouldn't work. Here he was offering her everything she'd been dreaming of since she'd met him—or at least the possibility of it. She wanted to take the leap, to grab on to this—to him—with both hands and not let go. And yet...

"Audrey?"

She hadn't answered him.

"I got the job at Berkeley." She said it automatically, because it impacted them, and he needed to know. But she knew at once that absolutely was not what he needed to hear right now.

Hudson pulled back. "Oh."

"I haven't accepted yet." She rushed to say it, wishing she could reel the conversation back a few clicks and take back her announcement, at least until she had a chance to think about the details, the ramifications.

"But you're planning to." It wasn't a question.

"I was. I'm supposed to fly back to California next week to meet with the department chair." But she'd made the plans without him in the equation. She'd had no idea he would come back, no idea he would want to pursue things with her beyond camp.

"Congratulations." Somehow, he managed to dig up a whisper of a smile, though his eyes were dark, devastated. It was like watching everything she'd built with him over the past weeks crumble.

"I can push it back. Take some more time for us to talk about this." She was a fucking prodigy. Surely, she could come up with a way to make this work. "Maybe we can—"

"No." There was no anger in his voice. Just a heart-wrenching resignation. "No, I think this is a sign." He reached out to skim a hand over her cheek. "I'm grateful I got the chance to know you."

Don't do this. Don't close this door.

But Audrey couldn't see an alternative. She *wanted* to get back to her career, needed to get back to a true mental challenge. That had been sorely missing in her life since the accident, and the prospect of having it back wasn't something she could walk away from. Even if money were no object, maintaining a long-distance relationship from one coast almost to the other was madness.

She couldn't ask him to leave his family, his friends, his life for the prospect of what might be between them. There was nothing she could say to give them any hope, and they both knew it.

Hudson held out his hand. "I want to dance with you."

Heart squeezing, Audrey took it. They went back to the boathouse, back to the noise and the people. As they stepped onto the dance floor, the music rolled into "The Time of My Life" from *Dirty Dancing*. How bittersweet and apropos. So many romantics watched that movie, convinced that Baby and Johnny stayed together. But Johnny hadn't come back to be with her. He'd come back to make things right for her with her father, and to make things right between them before they said goodbye. Because all that could ever be between those two people who lived in different worlds was that summer fling.

15

AS THE ENGINE ROLLED back up to the firehouse, Hudson leapt down, feeling amped up and ready to take on the world. His adrenaline was high in the wake of the second-story house fire. Three at home. No injuries. The structure itself wasn't a total loss. And he'd had no flashbacks. Not even a tremor. All in all, a good end to his first day back in the field.

Hudson accepted the handshakes and back slaps of the other members of his company.

Carlos Ortega grinned. "It's good to have you back, man."

"Good to be back, Cheech."

"You ready to do some real work after two weeks of lazing around?" This came from Luke

Hanover, aka Crash. He hauled out the hose, ready to spray down the engine.

"You remember *how* to do real work after all that?" Aaron Egerton taunted.

"Enough to recognize your lazy ass was on bathroom rotation, Sparky. Your mama'd be ashamed to think that's how you scrub a toilet."

"Sorry to disappoint you, Ma." He blew Hudson a kiss. "I'll get right on that."

Hudson shot up his middle finger and made the rookie laugh.

All around him, his fellow firefighters leapt into action, going through the usual post-fire routines of washing and refilling the truck, divvying up the paperwork, cleaning the turnout gear. As soon as the gear was dealt with, he hit the showers, rinsing off the acrid scent of smoke and sweat. It felt good to be back in the rhythm of the station, part of the crew. It felt good to be useful again.

"Chicken Little's making chili," Ortega announced as they dressed. "You should stick around for that. See the guys on B shift."

"I'll do that." Hudson pulled his phone from his locker and checked his messages.

Audrey: **How did the first day back go?**

And just like that, the yawning void he'd been trying to ignore became center focus again.

Missing her was different from missing John and Steve. They'd been an integral part of the fabric of his days for years. Being back here, even surrounded by the rest of his company, he felt a bit like he was operating without one of his arms. But he was learning to adapt, learning to depend on the others, even if they hadn't developed a life-long mind-meld. Trust was a necessary part of the job. But missing Audrey was a physical ache. Because she was still out there in the world. She just wasn't with him. How had she become such a part of him in only two weeks?

They'd had one last night together after the dance. Charlie had graciously made himself scarce, bunking elsewhere. They'd made the most of it. And instead of making love to her like it was the start of the rest of forever, he'd loved her like it was goodbye. Because it was. She'd tried to convince him it didn't have to be that way. They'd swapped contact information and promises to keep in touch. But each text, each call just ripped the scab off a wound that wasn't healing.

He wanted to hear her voice. To tell her about the day. Instead, he shoved the phone in his pocket without responding and headed for the kitchen. Jason Bradley stood at the stove, stirring a massive pot of chili. From the scents that were wafting his way, Hudson was guessing he'd gone for his four-pepper chili. He hoped like hell there was plenty of sour cream to tone down the heat. A few other guys stood around the table, noshing on tortilla chips and cheese dip.

Jason turned with a wide smile. "Good to see you back, Ma."

Hudson exchanged a back-thumping hug with the other man. "You cubs been behaving?"

"As much as ever. Have you met Hank O'Malley?"

"I haven't."

"Hank, this is Hudson Lowell, aka Ma. Hud, Hank. We call him Pogo. He's a transfer from Boston."

Hudson shook the other man's hand, appreciating that no one verbalized the awkward fact that he was here to replace John. "Decide you're tired of the big ass city?"

"Just wanted a change. The wife wanted to raise our kids in a smaller city."

The stab of envy was swift and unexpected. "How many you got?"

Pogo laughed. "None yet. But we're planning on three and enjoying the hell out of the practice."

As the joking took on a decidedly ribald air, Hudson's mind wandered. Transfer. For the first time since he'd watched Audrey ride away on that bus, he felt a flicker of hope. Maybe he could do with a change. He could fight fires anywhere. His primary reasons for staying here were gone. Maybe he could look into going to California. Would Audrey go for that? Surely, she would. She'd been the one who'd pushed to keep finding a way. Maybe this was it.

His fingers curled around the phone in his pocket just as it began to ring. Heart jolting, he checked the read out. Not Audrey.

"What's up, Rach?"

"Are you done with your shift?" There was a faintly panicked tone to her voice.

"Yeah. What's wrong?"

"My kitchen is flooded. I think the water supply to the dishwasher exploded."

"Did you turn off the main water line?"

She gave an alarmingly watery groan.

Dear God, please don't cry.

"No. John never showed me how. Where is it?"

Hudson gave a wave to the guys and headed for the door as he talked her through the process.

"Okay. I'm sorry to bother you with this, especially coming off a shift, but I could use a hand. And maybe a shop vac."

He felt his hope wink out as fast as it had lit.

How could he possibly think of leaving when Rachel was still here? With John gone, there was no one else to take care of her. He owed it to his friend to be there, to help her with whatever she needed. She had to come first.

"I'm on my way."

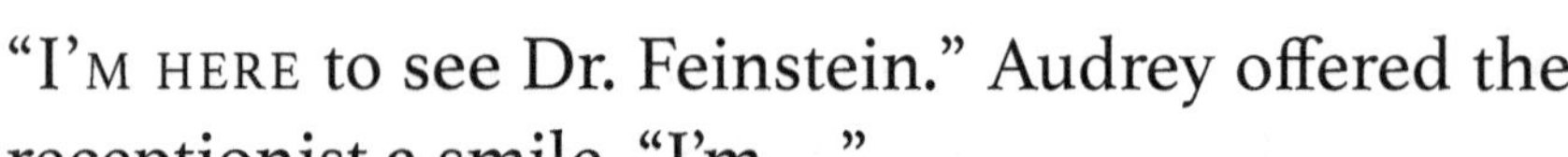

"I'M HERE to see Dr. Feinstein." Audrey offered the receptionist a smile. "I'm—"

The woman gave a curt nod that had the shellacked ash blonde curls of her short hair bobbing. "Dr. Graham. Of course. I remember you from your interview. Welcome back. He's tied up with someone just now. If you'll have a seat."

Audrey lowered herself into one of the low-backed waiting room chairs, rubbing absently at the ache in her legs. It had been a long flight from Tennessee. Whatever happened with this meeting, she needed a walk before she went back to the hotel. Pulling out the iPad she'd loaded with research literature, she tried to focus enough to read, but every discussion of survivor's guilt and PTSD had her thinking of Hudson.

Missing him was an ache that rivaled her legs. She hadn't heard from him. Not after the first few days. He'd said it was just too hard and asked for some distance. That had felt like a slap, but what else could she do? He deserved the right to move on. But it hadn't stopped her from thinking about him. She knew he'd gone back to work and was officially slated to be in the field again, taking fire calls. That was his version of getting back to real life. How was he handling it? She had to believe he was being safe, that he wouldn't be allowed back on duty if he was taking reckless risks. But she couldn't help thinking he needed more time to cope with everything that had happened.

"Dr. Graham!"

Audrey looked up as the department head crossed over to her, a broad smile creasing his bearded face. She carefully rose, holding in a wince as her knees protested the motion. "Dr. Feinstein, thank you for meeting with me." Audrey shook the older man's hand.

"Come on back."

She followed him into his office.

He took a seat behind a wide wooden desk, with an old-fashioned leather blotter, and steepled his hands. It was the gesture of a man who knew he was in charge of everything in his domain. "I do hope this visit means you've made your decision to join our faculty."

She'd run the numbers, weighed the pros and cons, and knew that this was the opportunity of a lifetime. But the decision wasn't as cut-and-dried as it might be for anyone else. She wasn't the same woman who'd interviewed here only a few weeks ago.

"May I be frank with you?"

An expression of surprise and perhaps a little concern flitted over his face. "Of course."

"When I interviewed, I explained that I left my position at Duke because I'd been in an accident, and during my protracted recovery, I could no longer perform my duties as expected."

"Yes. The committee discussed that. It's not a problem for us."

Audrey smiled a little. "I didn't think it was, or you wouldn't have offered me the job." She folded her hands. "I'd like to give you a little more detail."

"I assure you, it has no bearing on your hire-ability. If you need additional accommodations in the classroom or lab, we can make that happen."

"I appreciate that. But that's not why I want to tell you. My circumstances have direct bearing on my research interests, which I intend to shift from those discussed in my interview."

Feinstein looked intrigued. "Go on."

So, she told him, in broad strokes, about the

accident and her subsequent recovery. She'd intended to stop there, sticking to the logical, organized presentation she'd prepared on the flight. Keeping things as professional and clinically distant as possible. But her reasons for pursuing this *were* personal. Deeply so.

"When I left here a few weeks ago, I went to summer camp in the Berkshires."

"Summer camp?" He was clearly wondering where this was going.

Audrey waved that off. "Bucket list. Not the point. While I was there, I met the firefighter who rescued me."

When she'd finished, Feinstein sat back in his big leather chair. He was back to steepling his fingers. "That's...quite the story, Dr. Graham. And I can understand why you'd be moved to do further research in that area. However, that's not a good fit for our department. Perhaps, in a few years, once you've re-established yourself, you can look at branching off—provided you acquire grant funding, of course."

Audrey didn't want to wait years. She didn't want to go back to her old, heartless research. "I appreciate your honesty. But the fact is, this is what I want now. If my accident taught me nothing else, it's that there is no guarantee of tomorrow. I need to do this. I need to shift my research to something that stands to directly impact people in a positive way. I need to make a difference, and I can't do that unless I make a move to applied sociology. I'm not willing to go back to the hours and insanity of tenure track academia unless it's for something I'm passionate about. Life's too short. So, this is what I'm going to pursue." Somewhere. "I understand if you wish to withdraw the offer.

He had a good poker face—no one made department head in academia without it—but she could tell she'd shocked him. What rising academic in their right mind would turn down what they were offering her?

Dr. Feinstein was quiet for a long time, clearly weighing his words. "If that's how you really feel, Dr. Graham, I'm afraid we don't have a place for you at this time."

She'd expected this. But the confirmation still knocked her back and made her grateful for the support of her chair. Some part of her was screaming, *Are you crazy? You can't walk away from this opportunity!* Audrey ignored it, leaning over to grab her purse from the floor. "I completely understand. And I apologize for wasting your and the committee's time." She started to rise.

"Wait. You also have a Masters in clinical psychology, do you not?"

It was the last thing she'd expected him to ask. "I haven't used it for anything, and I'm not licensed to practice, but yes."

"I have a colleague who'd be very interested in speaking with you. Rhona Prescott over at Syracuse."

Audrey's breath caught. "But their department isn't hiring." She'd checked that from the airport as she and Sam waited on their flight back to Tennessee.

"She's not in the sociology department. She's a research professor—part of a joint program with the VA hospital there. I think she'd really appreciate your story." He picked up the phone. "Let me make a call."

16

AUDREY WAS GREEN BY the time she arrived at the firehouse. That hadn't been the plan, but she'd been more optimistic than she should've been about driving down I-81 for the first time since the accident. Maybe she should've taken a circuitous route through the city instead of the interstate. Too late now. She'd fought off the panic attack, so to her mind, the whole experience had been a win. Except for the fact that she was clammy with anxiety sweat and still feeling nauseous. Only some of that was from the panic attack.

It seemed her chest had been tight from the moment the bus had left Camp Firefly Falls. As if she couldn't quite take a full breath away from Hudson. Stupid. But the sensation hadn't gone away. It had been three weeks since she'd had any contact with him. Three weeks during which she'd moved heaven and earth. Three weeks in which she'd changed her whole life.

It would be worth it. It had to be.

She climbed out of her car and smoothed her hands over the skirt that was already smooth, then strode toward the four-bay fire station. One of the bay doors was up, and she cautiously stepped inside. "Hello?"

A head popped out from behind the big truck in front of her. "Help you ma'am?"

"I'm looking for Hudson Lowell."

The young man, who couldn't have been more than twenty, came toward her, wiping his hands on a towel. "He's not here."

"Oh." Flummoxed, Audrey just stood there. She'd been so busy rehearsing what she wanted to say, she hadn't given any thought to the fact that he might've changed shifts or taken a day off. Or what if going back out on calls hadn't worked? What if he'd had a relapse of his PTSD symptoms?

Another man stepped out of a room off to the side. "What's going on?"

The young guy jerked a thumb in her direction. "She's looking for Ma."

Ma? "Beg your pardon?" Audrey asked.

"Hudson."

"You call him Ma?"

The second man strode over and flashed a grin. "Nickname. Because he's always taking care of everybody, like a den mother."

"Yeah, he's good about that," she said, and ached. "I'll just call him. Thanks." She'd wanted to surprise him.

That's not why you didn't call in the first place.

She'd been afraid he wouldn't answer, or, worse, he'd tell her he didn't want to see her.

As Audrey turned to leave, a woman dressed in cargo pants and an SFD t-shirt materialized from somewhere. She gave Audrey the once over. "He's up at the picnic."

"Picnic?"

"Yeah, the department's sponsoring a big picnic for the Fourth. He was on first shift here this morning so he could attend this afternoon."

Suddenly Audrey felt stupid. It was the Fourth of July. She'd been so focused on everything else, she hadn't considered the holiday. He'd be with family and friends, probably. Busy. Surrounded by people. Her belly clutched again.

He's going to want to see you. You're not coming all this way and chickening out.

She squared her shoulders. "Where?"

They gave her directions. Twenty minutes later, she finally found parking and began the hike through the park, looking for a familiar set of broad shoulders. Scents of grilling meat and fried dough permeated the air. As the nausea faded, her stomach began to growl, reminding her it was coming up on dinner. But she didn't want to meet Hudson again with a hot dog or funnel cake in her hands.

There were people everywhere. Families. Children. Clusters of friends. Lines snaked out from vendor tents and assorted games. How would she ever find him amid this crowd? She set up a mental grid and began to crisscross the park, methodically scanning faces. Daylight was fading. All around her, people were setting up lawn chairs and blankets, talking about the fireworks to come. She was running out of time. Maybe she should just give up until tomorrow. Call him like a sane person. Wrestling with disappointment, she turned back toward the parking lot.

And there he was. Smiling. With a tall, willowy blonde in his arms.

Audrey stopped dead, her stomach dropping

to her toes, her chest cranking like a vise. After everything they'd shared, everything he'd said, she hadn't expected he could move on so fast. But they had no understanding. They'd had no future. There was nothing stopping him from finding a rebound, moving on to someone else.

Pulling back from his embrace, the blonde saw her first. Her brows shot up, and she said something to Hudson. He turned, surprise flickering over his face. Audrey couldn't make herself move, not to approach him and not to retreat. Her heart beat an erratic tattoo against her ribs and her palms went damp.

Hudson said something to his companions—because of course he was with a group. His family, probably. And everybody was staring at her. He made it over to her in less than a dozen strides. There was no quick, impulsive hug, no kiss hello. He looked...guarded and wary.

"Hi," she managed, hating the catch in her voice.

"Hi, yourself."

Audrey knew she was staring and couldn't seem to stop. She drank in the sight of him, absorbing the snug fit of his gray t-shirt across his broad, capable shoulders, and the faint shadow of stubble on his solid jaw. Her tongue felt thick and clumsy, and the carefully prepared speech she'd been rehearsing simply disappeared. "God, it's good to see you."

She wanted to throw herself into his arms, but he didn't look happy to see her. He didn't look angry either. Audrey didn't know what to do with this neutrality. She couldn't read him, and that made her anxiety crank higher. Maybe this was a mistake.

Hudson jerked his head. "Come and meet my family."

The nerves ratcheted up another notch as he led her over to the group, who looked on with undisguised curiosity.

"Everybody, this is Audrey Graham."

Half a dozen people nodded or waved at her.

Hudson reeled off introductions, most of which Audrey was too rattled to catch. He gestured to the blonde he'd been hugging. "And this is Rachel."

John's widow. Audrey glanced at Hudson and got a tiny confirmatory nod. So maybe that hadn't been what she'd thought. Still, none of this was going how she'd planned.

Use your manners. "Pleased to meet you all."

"I'm thrilled to meet you." Rachel stepped in, giving Audrey a hard hug.

Startled, Audrey could only stand there, wooden, as the other woman squeezed.

"Thank you for giving him back to us," she whispered.

Nothing in her repository of proper social behavior seemed the right response to that, so she gave Rachel an awkward half-hug in return. "You're welcome?"

"Hudson's told me so much about you," Rachel continued, stepping back as if they hadn't just shared one of the world's most awkward hugs.

Uncertain, Audrey glanced at Hudson, but he was still doing an impression of a stone wall.

Hudson's mom, Janie, smiled. "How do you know Hudson, dear?"

"That's...a little complicated. Your son saved my life two years ago."

Predictably, several pairs of eyes flicked downward to the legs left exposed by her summer sundress. Hudson briefly pressed a hand to the small of her back. The automatic gesture of support and reassurance loosened some of the knots in her stomach.

"We reconnected at camp," she finished, feeling lame and awkward and wishing they could go somewhere private to talk.

Before she could ask him, the younger woman

—Hudson's sister?—asked, "What brings you to Syracuse?"

Audrey didn't want to get into this with a crowd. She had so much she needed to say to him, to explain. But they were all looking at her, waiting for some kind of answer. "Business." The word tripped from her tongue automatically and felt wrong. It hadn't been business that had brought her to Syracuse.

"Oh yeah? What do you do?" Janie asked.

"She's a research professor at Berkeley," Hudson replied. There was a curious mix of pride and strain in his tone.

Audrey met his eyes. "No, I'm not." She wanted to get that out there as fast as possible, since telling him about Berkeley in the first place had been the moment she'd felt what was between them fracture.

It was only as Hudson went utterly still that she realized he'd been practically vibrating with nervous energy. "What do you mean you're not?"

"I went to California. Once I told them about the change in my direction of research, they didn't want me."

A crease appeared between his brows. Audrey wanted to kiss it smooth. "I don't understand. They already offered you the job."

"They offered me a job based on a continuation of the research I began at Duke. They weren't interested in applied sociology, and at this point, I'm not willing to do anything else." This was more than she'd meant to say in front of their audience, but she had Hudson's undivided attention now and knew she couldn't leave him hanging.

"I've been in mainstream academia my entire career. Hell, my entire life. After the accident, all I could think about was getting back on track. Then I met you. And you made me want—" *You.* "—something different. Something more. So, I left California, and I came here."

"Here?" The word was sharp, and she could see the lines of tension beneath his carefully blank expression.

"The thing about academia is that it's a terribly small world. The department chair at Berkeley put me in touch with a former colleague of his—Rhoda Prescott. She holds a joint appointment between Syracuse University and the VA hospital. She's starting a new program working with veterans on coping with PTSD and reintegration into society. I convinced her to hire me to develop a new branch of the program on coping with survivor's guilt."

A muscle jumped in Hudson's jaw.

Audrey felt a flutter of panic. What if he didn't understand? What if he thought her shift in research was because she thought he was damaged? That she thought she could fix him?

She knotted her hands. "I meant what I told you before, that I couldn't imagine going back to the rigors of academia unless it was for something that really mattered. I want to help people. You just helped me figure out the focus."

Hudson was staring at her. "So, you walked away from a shot at Berkeley, changed your entire research focus, practically produced a job out of thin air, and turned your entire life on its ear—because of me?"

Her knees felt loose and her stomach dipped like she was at the top of a precipice. "Do you remember what you said to me that day at the top of the ropes course?"

"You'll have to take the leap."

Audrey nodded once and spread her hands, feeling exposed and vulnerable and more terrified than she'd been in her entire life. "I'm taking it. No guidewire, no safety harness, no net." *Oh please, catch me.*

Tension radiated off him in waves, but still, he said nothing.

She swallowed. "If you've changed your mind, I understand. We haven't even talked in—"

She didn't finish the thought, didn't finish the breath, because suddenly his hands were buried in her hair and his mouth was a fever on hers. All the days and all the miles of distance evaporated. Heart leaping, she fisted her hands in his shirt and kissed him back—at least until the applause and whistles started. Blood rushing to her cheeks, she broke away, feeling twin urges to laugh and cry with relief.

"Twenty-six days," he breathed.

Audrey blinked at him. "What?"

"Since we last talked. Twenty-six days, nine hours, and somewhere around forty minutes, give or take. I'm not sure what time you got here. Time kinda stopped." His eyes warmed with a smile, like the sun sparking off the surface of the ocean. "I've been counting."

The clamp around her chest loosened, and she took her first full breath in a month. Relief had her sagging against him.

Hudson tightened his hold, taking her weight. "You okay?"

"So okay. It's just, you've melted my knees again." She aimed for a stern expression and missed by a mile, unable to repress a grin. "Terrible habit of yours."

His smile was blinding. "Who needs knees anyway? You've got me."

And that, Audrey thought, as he kissed her again, hard and fast, was everything she'd ever needed.

EPILOGUE

THE CAMP FIREFLY FALLS bus was pulling out of the gravel lot as Hudson turned into it. People were milling everywhere, cheerfully greeting old friends and bouncing between the stack of luggage that had been offloaded and the registration table.

Rachel took one look at the chaos and said, "Maybe this was a bad idea."

What a difference a year makes, Hudson mused as he climbed out of the Jeep. "It's a great idea. You need some time away, just like I did."

His cousin turned fretful eyes toward Audrey. "But I hate to leave you with the group all by yourself."

Audrey smiled and took Rachel by the arms. "The group will be *fine*. All the new guys are doing great. They're taking to the baking like ducks to water."

Who knew that a bunch of taciturn, struggling, ex-military men would find new purpose as bakers, of all things? Well, Audrey had. She'd co-opted Rachel's commercial baking expertise and pioneered a new reintegration program involving a combination of skills training and therapy. The pilot study had shown great promise—enough that Audrey had landed a five-year grant to evaluate the program more in depth.

"But—" Rachel began.

"No buts. I've got this," Audrey told her firmly. "You've been pulling the workaholic routine for a year. It's time for a break and Camp Firefly Falls is the perfect opportunity. You're going to love it."

To settle the issue, Hudson hauled Rachel's massive duffel to the registration table, where Heather Tully sat with her clipboard and a mile-wide smile.

"Hudson! I didn't know you were joining us again this summer."

"I'm not. My cousin is. Rachel McCleary. We're dropping her off."

"We?" Heather asked.

Audrey ducked under his arm and snuggled close. "We."

"Audrey! How good to see you. I'd ask how you're doing, but it's obvious you're happy. You're glowing."

"They're disgustingly happy," Rachel put in with a smile. "It's adorable."

It had taken Hudson a while to get accustomed to her enthusiastic support of his relationship with Audrey. He'd worried that being openly in love around her would make John's absence that much more apparent. But while she'd grieved hard and long, she'd made it abundantly clear that seeing him happy was helping her heal. It hadn't hurt that she and Audrey had become fast friends.

Hudson made introductions. "I trust you'll take good care of her while she's here."

"Of course, we will." Heather handed over the welcome packet and began giving the spiel. "One of our staff will take you to your cabin." She waved and a familiar blond guy trotted over.

"Charlie!" Audrey broke away to give Charlie a big hug.

Charlie grinned as he hugged her back. "Well, I'll be damned. Y'all worked it out."

"We did, indeed."

Hudson chuckled to himself. *Greet old friends at camp.* She was getting to cross something else off her list. There weren't too many things left. It had been one of his greatest pleasures to make sure of that as she'd settled into her new life in Syracuse. Sometime around Christmas he'd started his own list of things he wanted to see and do with her. He was hoping he'd be crossing the first one off today.

"What are you doing as staff?" he asked.

"I have left the book business." Charlie said it in a tone that clearly implied, *It's complicated.* "Since I was at loose ends for the summer, I thought being a counselor here was a good chance to re-evaluate my life and figure out what's next."

"Seems like that's going around," Rachel muttered.

"Camp is good for that," Audrey declared.

And thank God for it. He didn't really want to think where he'd be if Audrey hadn't come back into his life.

"I wish you two were going to be here with me," Rachel pouted.

Audrey squeezed her tight. "I know. Me, too. We'll schedule far enough out for next summer that we can all get time off. Meanwhile, you have a *great* time! Don't do anything I wouldn't do."

"You did everything while you were here," Hudson reminded her.

Audrey grinned. "Exactly."

Hudson hugged Rachel himself, hoping Camp Firefly Falls was as good an experience for her as it had been for him. "Have fun. We'll see you in two weeks."

Charlie hefted Rachel's bag and made a sweeping gesture toward the trail. "After you, madam."

They said their goodbyes. Audrey looked at the trails leading up to camp proper, her expression full of nostalgia. "I really do wish we'd been able to come this summer."

Hudson laced his hands behind her back. "Want to take a walk around the lake before we get back on the road? Stretch your legs?"

"Oh, that sounds good. And maybe we can stop at Boone's for a slice of pie on the way home?" She turned those big, baby blues on him, and he was a goner.

"Anything you want."

They took the trail up to camp, around the lodge, on past the boathouse to the pier. It looked exactly the same as last summer, but he felt so totally different. All because of this woman.

Hudson tugged her back against him, pressing a kiss to the top of her head as they looked out over the sparkling water of Lake Waawaatesi. "You know, I was standing right here the first time I saw you last summer."

"When I followed you out from the dance."

"No. I saw you from across the lake. Right over there." He pointed to the trail, where a trio of women walked and talked, their laughter floating on the breeze. "You were taking a walk, probably stretching your legs like today, and I envied you."

"Why?"

"You looked so contented and peaceful. And I was so...not." He turned her to face him. "But you gave me that. You pulled me out of myself and taught me that living isn't just the best way to honor my friends, it's the brave choice. You always make the brave choice. And that makes you *my* hero."

Her eyes were already glimmering with emotion. "Hudson. All I did was love you."

"It's the best thing that's ever happened to me. You're the best thing that's ever happened to me. The past year with you has been the best of my life. That's why I brought you back up here today. It felt like it had to be here."

"What does?"

"The beginning of everything." Hudson took a step back, dropping to one knee and pulling the ring box from his cargo shorts. "I love you, Audrey. I want to make a life, a family with you. To grow old with you. Say you'll marry me. Be my wife, my everything."

Audrey pressed a hand to her mouth. The tears spilled over and Hudson's stomach bottomed out. Maybe it was too soon. Maybe doing it here was a mistake. Maybe—

"Yes." She dropped her hands and reached for him, her smile beaming like the sun. "Yes, I'll marry you."

Relief burst through him, and he surged to his feet, scooping her off hers with a celebratory whoop. Applause and cheers broke out from somewhere behind them. Hudson stopped spinning to see that several dozen people lined the bank. Charlie and Rachel were at the head of the pack.

Charlie cupped a hand around his mouth. "Kiss!"

Rachel picked up the cry, until the entire pack was chanting it.

Audrey laughed and lifted her face to his. "Better give the people what they want."

"You already gave me what I wanted," he said, and closed the distance.

~

Choose Your Next Romance

I wrote this book back in 2018 as part of a shared world project that has since disbanded. I was always sad there weren't more summer camp stories, so I decided to change that! Second Chance Summer is now the first in a brand new trilogy! Book 2, *Summer Camp Secret,* releases April 12th. But while you're waiting...

After watching her BFF fall in love, I *know* you want to hear about Sam! She's actually a second chance romance and her story is a twofer. She's got a SECRET from Vegas that nobody knows about, not even Audrey. You can read all about that in *Until We Meet Again.* But her present day story is all about a second chance with a Marine who's never forgotten her. Grab that story in *Come A Little Closer.*

Or maybe you're waiting for Rachel? She gets her happily ever after in *Stirred Up by a SEAL* Book 3 of the Bad Boy Bakers series, which follows the graduates from Audrey's baking therapy program!

It begins with *Mixed Up With a Marine*, and you can read Mia and Brax's backstory prequel *Rescued By a Bad Boy* for FREE because I'm all about those second chance romances.

Keep turning pages to get a sneak peek of *Summer Camp Secret!*

SNEAK PEEK SUMMER CAMP SECRET

Pretending to be the fiancée of some random guy in a bar isn't the kind of thing Aspen Fairchild would normally do. Ever. But when a medical scare sends her reeling onto a path of "live life to its fullest," and she sees an opportunity to do a good deed, she figures she can use all the good karma she can get.

Pro hockey player Brooks Hennessey was just taking time off, working through his grief, trying to do a good deed. But now his fake engagement has gone viral, and his publicist wants to know what he's going to do about it.

He knows what he'd like to do: spend his week at grown-up summer camp with the woman he can't stop thinking about.

She knows what she'd like to do: spend her week at Camp Firefly Falls with the guy who unexpectedly rocked her world.

But the girl of his dreams is hiding something, keeping him at arm's length. Because the guy who makes her heart beat is oh-so-vulnerable to the last thing she'd want to burden him with. Will she give them a chance, or will she run away before he can learn her summer camp secret?

Grab this steamy contemporary summer romance about a fake engagement, real attraction, and the secrets people keep when they're trying to protect those they love.

~

*W*hy didn't I go with the sticky boobs?

Aspen Fairchild shifted in her seat, trying desperately to get some relief from the strapless bra that had gone rogue and apparently popped an underwire. Said wire was currently poking the underside of her left breast as if it intended to hold her hostage until the end of the wedding ceremony. She didn't dare try to adjust anything. Not while the photographer was snapping away, capturing the processional only a few feet from her position on the front row. So, she pasted on a smile she hoped didn't look like a grimace and tried desperately to focus on the happy occasion.

And it was a happy occasion.

A dozen feet away, beneath a simple, white wooden archway festooned with chiffon and accented with clusters of flowers, strands of pearls and crystals that shimmered in the fading sunlight, stood her father, Walter, waiting for his bride. As Tricia reached the head of the simple driftwood aisle and took his hand, he beamed bright enough to rival the setting sun. The nerves and the joy made him look at least ten years younger than his fifty-one years. Aspen hadn't known he could still be that kind of happy. She sure as hell hadn't seen him look like this since before they'd lost her mother to an aggressive form of breast cancer ten years before.

There'd been such a fast turnaround from her mom's diagnosis, to being told it was terminal, to having to say goodbye. There'd been no long, lingering sickness. No wasting away. No chance to adjust. It had been fast and brutal. Mere weeks. Then she'd been gone. Gillian's death had absolutely leveled them both. Aspen and her father had spent the past decade propping each other up because life hadn't turned out the way they'd expected, and neither of them quite knew what to do in a world without her mother.

Then he'd met Tricia Rogers, a divorced mom of two who'd been cautiously getting back out there after her youngest had flown the nest for college. Given the distance between Cooper's Bend, in the mountains of north Georgia, and Savannah, where Tricia lived, Aspen had been skeptical. But they'd made it work, and here they were, eighteen months later, tying the knot in a beachside ceremony on Tybee Island in front of family and friends.

"Dearly beloved, we are gathered here today..."

As the vows began, Aspen was painfully aware of how empty the groom's side was. A handful of her father's friends had made the trek from home, but she was the only blood family he had left. Tricia's side was bursting with people. Her two kids, her mother, some siblings, cousins, and a multitude of friends that proved how integrated she was into her community. The disparity made it crystal clear how little was holding her father in Cooper's Bend. They hadn't discussed where he and Tricia would be living. Aspen hadn't been able to bring herself to ask, because neither alternative was comfortable. Either he sold the house and moved down to Savannah with his new wife, far away from Aspen, or he moved Tricia into the home he'd shared with Gillian and inevitably changed the rooms that had become calcified with memory. Both options hurt. But Aspen wouldn't say a word to dim this hard-won happiness for her father. He deserved this second chance at love, no matter what it meant for her.

"I now pronounce you husband and wife. You may kiss the bride!"

Walter bent Tricia back in a dip made all the more dramatic against the magnificent sunset sky. Aspen led the cheers and applause, even as the bra continued to molest her. First chance she got, she was slipping away to a bathroom to deal with the thing. Even if that meant stripping it off and shoving it into the trash. It had been a hot day that was leading into what would certainly be a warm night. Maybe no one would notice her girls gone wild in the halter dress.

But the opportunity kept eluding her. In the

wake of the ceremony, she got pulled in for family photos with the happy couple. Guests swarmed for more photos before the light faded. Aspen thought for sure she'd have a chance to get away as they all walked en masse through the sun-warmed sand up the beach to the resort where the reception was being held. But the wedding planner snagged her to ask a question about the cake cutting. Then Heidi and Everett, her brand new step-siblings, insisted she needed to contribute to the playlist for the reception. And somehow, she found herself seated for the meal without ever being able to get a moment alone.

As the food was served, she crossed her arms and tried to surreptitiously readjust things. That only forced the bra into escape mode, inching down her torso. The whole thing made her think of her mom, who used to say, "Strapless bras are like very rude and forward men. They start at the top and quickly work their way down."

The memory made her want to snicker, as she had during the prom dress shopping trip when Gillian had shared that little gem.

Definitely should've gone with the sticky boobs. Though Aspen hadn't been sure that they'd stay stuck, given the humidity of south Georgia in July.

By the time they'd made it through the meal

and into the speeches, the recalcitrant bra was barely covering her nipples. On the plus side, the tender spot that had been abused for the past couple of hours was getting a bit of a break. As soon as the attention was off the head table, she was saying to hell with it and dashing for the bathroom.

From his place at the center of the long table, her father rose and took the microphone. He looked so dashing in his tuxedo, his salt and pepper hair ruffled by the ocean breeze.

"My dear friends and family, I can't tell you how overjoyed I am that all of you could join us tonight to celebrate with Tricia and me here on beautiful Tybee Island. This is a second chance at love that neither of us expected, and we're so excited to start our new life together as husband and wife."

Despite the pang in her chest, Aspen clapped along with the rest of the guests as he lifted Tricia's hand to his lips.

"To that end, some of you may be surprised to learn that I'll be moving to Savannah to join Tricia."

Aspen's breath wooshed out as if he'd sucker punched her. That was it then. The answer she'd been afraid he'd choose. Two more goodbyes she wasn't prepared to make.

"But Cooper's Bend will always hold such special memories for me. It was where I raised my beautiful daughter, Aspen. As such, while I start this new chapter, I can't imagine a better person to inherit the house there than her."

Wait. What?

Walter turned to face her, the green eyes he'd passed onto her shining with emotion. "Which is why it brings me so much pride to announce that I'm passing the house onto you, for you to make your own memories there, and maybe raise a family of your own someday. Aspen, sweetheart, you are the light of my life, and I know you'll fill that house with joy and laughter for years to come."

"Dad..." Aspen could barely get the words out past the lump in her throat. Relief made her limbs shake as she pushed herself up from the chair and moved to hug him.

His arms closed around her, warm and firm. An anchor when she needed one the most. "It wouldn't have been right for it to go to anyone but you."

"Thank you." Her voice came out barely above a whisper, and she was deathly afraid her waterproof mascara was about to be put to the test.

They stood in a swaying hug for a long minute, lost in their private bittersweet moment. Then the DJ started up music and called for the first dance.

Walter stepped back. "You gonna dance with your old man after this?"

Aspen sniffed back the tears that wanted to fall. "Absolutely. Go on. Tricia's waiting."

He bussed her cheek, then took his wife's hand and led her onto the dance floor.

Aspen couldn't wait any longer. She made a break for it, weaving her way through the tables and inside the resort to the bathroom. Bypassing the little seating area for women to take a few minutes to rest, she locked herself into a stall. For a long moment, she stood, hands braced against the door as she wrestled with emotion.

He was giving her the house. It was an amazing gift on so many fronts. He was moving, but he wasn't taking the last of her mother away from her. Letting her make the choice about what and how to change things. Knowing she needed that connection for a while longer. Beyond all that, the house was paid for, free and clear. Being able to move back in and avoid the burden of rent would give her the financial freedom to do... well, she didn't know what, because she hadn't ever had that kind of flexibility. Maybe she'd finally think about stretching some the wings that had been clipped by her mother's death.

And that's all stuff to think about later. Right now, it's time to burn this bra.

Reaching back, she released the clasp and wiggled the offending lingerie out of her dress. The moment her breasts were free, she heaved a sigh of relief. God, that felt good. Bras had to have been a torture device invented by men. She examined the edge and found that not only had the underwire poked through, it had straight up broken in two.

"Free nippies, it is." She slid a hand into the bodice of her dress and massaged the abused boob, hoping to relieve some of the ache. The tissue on the underside was swollen and irritated.

Damned bastard bra.

Except... no, this wasn't just an irritated spot. She dropped the bra to the floor and used both hands to palpitate the flesh. There was a decided lump deep in the tissue of her breast.

Terror struck like a viper, stealing the strength from her legs.

She had a lump in her breast.

Just like her mother.

She pressed a hand to her mouth to hold back the scream welling up in her chest.

No. No, no, no. This can't be happening.

They'd found Gillian's lump when she was forty.

Aspen was only twenty-eight.

The exterior door opened, and female laughter floated inside as other guests came in to check their makeup or use the facilities. The sound jolted her back to herself.

This was her father's wedding. He was out there, waiting to dance with her. To celebrate his new beginning. She wasn't about to say or do anything that would ruin his day. Not now. Not until she saw a doctor and had a diagnosis confirmed. There was absolutely nothing she could do about this before Monday morning.

Aspen took another few minutes to get herself under control. Then she trashed the bra and strode back out to the party to dance with her father, in case it was the last time she ever had a chance to do it.

FROM SOMEWHERE BENEATH the depths of the covers, Brooks Hennessy registered the pounding on his door. He was done dealing with all the things. The funeral had been endured. Condolences had been accepted. Casseroles had been frozen. All the aftermath crap had been dealt with. It was the off-season. He had no further professional obligations. The death certificate had arrived yesterday. He had every right to hole up in his house for another two months, until time for pre-season training.

The pounding came again, louder this time.

Brooks tugged the comforter up over his head. If he didn't respond, they would go away.

Even as the thought crossed his mind, he heard the sound of the door opening.

Dammit, he should never have given them spare keys to his place.

The murmur of low voices sounded as they moved through the house. He knew what they'd see. A riot of empty takeout containers and beer bottles, endless stacks of dirty dishes, and mountains of unopened mail. He hadn't been planning on company. If they had a problem with it, they could kiss his ass.

"Shit, dude." The shock in Colter Coughlin's tone had Brooks hunching his shoulders.

"Go away."

Grady Prichard, the third member of their trio, slapped a hand on Brooks's leg on top of the blanket. "Can't do that, man. We're here to make sure that you're doing the bare minimum to take care of yourself."

"I'm fine."

Brooks wasn't even in the same country as fine, but he wasn't about to admit that.

"Somehow, we don't believe you."

Brooks sensed them on either side of the foot of the bed seconds before the duvet was yanked off him. He sat up, glaring. "You're lucky I wasn't naked under here."

Grady rolled his eyes. "Nothing we haven't seen before in the locker room."

"Speaking of which, you need to go shower."

Brooks transferred his scowl to Colter. "Go away."

His buddy didn't blink. "Not gonna happen. At least, not until you've showered, and we've seen you eat something."

Knowing them well enough to ascertain the truth of this statement, Brooks swung his legs out of the bed and sat up. His whole body hurt. He hadn't been keeping up with the workouts that maintained his physique as a pro athlete. Not even the low-level ones that were his habit during the off season. What was the point? He wasn't even sure if he wanted to go back. So he felt about a hundred years old as he stood and moved toward his friends. Grady made a Vanna White gesture toward the open bathroom door. "Please enjoy. We'll help take care of the rest."

"Leave it," Brooks growled.

Colter slapped a hand on his shoulder and squeezed. "Just go shower, man. It'll make you feel a little more human."

Not having the energy to argue, Brooks stumbled into the bathroom to do as they ordered. As he stripped out of his T-shirt and basketball shorts, he had to admit he did smell like something that had been left to molder in the back of his locker over the course of a full season. Kind of like the lucky socks he'd worn during his AHL career before moving up to the pros. He stepped under the spray and let it beat down on his head and shoulders, loosening up muscles gone stiff with inactivity. He stayed in the bathroom longer than necessary, with a vague hope that his friends would have disappeared by the time he came out.

No such luck. When he stepped into his living room, dressed in clean sweatpants and a T-shirt, they'd done their best impression of Merry Maids. All the takeout containers and empty beer bottles had been cleared away. The low rumble of the dishwasher told him they'd dealt with the dishes as well.

Colter eyed him from head to toe. "Well now, you look a little bit more like someone who's part of the land of the living." The moment the words were out of his mouth, Colter winced. "Sorry. But do you feel better?"

"Set the bar lower, man." Brooks's gaze slid to the counter, where he spied a large pizza box. "Is that pizza from Tremoni's?" He didn't want to be interested, but the scent of tomatoes and garlic and grease had his stomach growling.

When was the last time he'd eaten?

"An extra-large pie, just for you." Grady nudged over a plate. "Eat."

Brooks recognized an order when he heard one, but he didn't have enough energy to ignore it in the name of being contrary. He opened the box and lifted out a slice covered in pepperoni, peppers, onions, and mushrooms. This would be the closest he'd come to a vegetable in at least a week. He bit in, closing his eyes as the spicy sauce and melted cheese hit his tongue.

"He is responding to normal stimuli. This is improvement," Colter declared.

Brooks just fixed a flat gaze on his friend. He finished the first slice of pizza, washing it down with filtered water from the fridge. The food did help a little. "Thanks."

As he reached for another slice, his friends exchanged a look. "Do I look that bad?"

This time it was Grady who grabbed his shoulder. "You really don't want us to answer that. But you do look better since the shower. Even if your beard is making you look like a homeless Viking."

Fresh irritation prickled. "You've done your wellness check, seen that I've showered and eaten. You're free to go anytime."

"That's not what friends do, Hennessy. We want to be here for you."

Colter nodded. "Yeah, you've done the hermit routine long enough. It's time you start getting out in the world again."

"If either of you think that I have any intention of going down to Denver in search of a puck bunny at one of our usual haunts, you are sorely mistaken." The last thing Brooks wanted to do was go out in public and risk being recognized. He was the reason his team had been kicked out of the playoffs. It was possible that the commentators had moved on to something else by now, but he had no interest in putting that theory to the test.

Colter looked to Grady. The Canadian had no poker-face to speak of, and Brooks could easily see the concern underlying his attempt at discretion.

"What is it?"

"We're just here to check on you," Colter insisted.

But Brooks wasn't reassured. A little frisson of unease trickled down his spine. "What?"

Grady sighed. "We overheard Maxwell talking."

Damien Maxwell was the general manager for their team. If they'd overheard something he was saying, the only thing that would be of any interest would be about Brooks's fate on the team. "What did he say?"

"He's looking to trade you. "

Brooks waited for the emotional sucker punch to hit. This was his pro-hockey career at stake. The thing he'd devoted his entire adult life to. The reason his mother hadn't felt as if she could tell him that she was sick.

But the blow never landed. He lifted his shoulder in a shrug. "And?"

"We just thought you'd want to know." Colter didn't seem to have any idea what to do with his lack of reaction. Another worried glance passed between his friends.

To prove he wasn't bothered, Brooks picked up another slice of pizza. "It's to be expected after I blew the playoffs." In truth, he should never have gotten back on the ice after his mother's death. His heart hadn't been in it. But his team had been counting on him. And he'd screwed the pooch in a big way. Maxwell was well within his rights and his duty to the team in discussing trades with other teams.

"Do you know who he's negotiating with?"

"No. Yanovich ran us off before we could hear more."

Brooks shrugged again. "It doesn't matter. If he's looking to trade me, I'll get traded. I'll either go, or I'll retire."

Colter straightened. "Shit, dude. Would you really retire?"

Grady frowned so hard a line formed between his dark brows. "Yeah. I know you're in a bad way right now, but this is your career."

The career Brooks was no longer certain he wanted.

He wasn't angry with Maxwell. This was the

nature of pro hockey. He'd known that when he signed contracts in the beginning nearly a decade ago. If he expected to feel something at the prospect of leaving Colorado, he was mistaken. All he felt was numb.

"What am I supposed to do about it?"

If his friends were offended that he wasn't making an effort to prove that he wanted to stay, or that he valued their friendship, they didn't show it. Instead, Grady braced his elbows on the counter. "We expect you to take care of yourself. Above the team, above us, we want to know that you're okay."

The idea of it was laughable. Not the thought that his friends cared—he certainly appreciated that, no matter how much he was growling at them—but the idea that he would ever be okay again in a world without his mother. A world where he hadn't been able to say goodbye.

"That's a tall order, man."

"We know. That's why we think it would do you good to get out of town for a bit. Take a little vacation."

"A vacation? You think I want to go visit a beach or some shit right now?"

Colter spoke up. "Not a beach. We were thinking the mountains. The middle of the woods. Something to suit your current grizzly bear personality." He softened the teasing with a little bit of a smile.

"The middle of the woods might not be so terrible," he conceded. He'd be far away from reporters and the not-so-well-meaning public who thought his grief was for their consumption.

"Good." Grady straightened with a nod. "We've already booked you a cabin in the Berkshires."

Brooks blinked. "You did what now?"

"We booked you a week-long stay at a grown-up summer camp on the other side of the country. You've been away from New York for long enough that you shouldn't be as easily recognizable over there as you are here. It should give you the privacy you want with the amenities of a resort. Let someone else see to the laundry and the cleaning and the food so you don't have to."

"It's called Camp Firefly Falls," Colter added. "Apparently it used to be a sleep-away camp for kids a long time ago, but some former campers bought it and turned it into a resort a few years ago."

Brooks was still staring. "You're sending me to summer camp?"

"You need a break. An all-inclusive resort somewhere tropical is not your jam, so this seemed like the next best option." Grady put an envelope on the counter. "All the information about it is in here. The only thing you've gotta do is book a flight to get to that side of the country. Your reservation starts end of next week."

"You expect me to just up and drop everything to fly across the country to go to summer camp?"

Grady arched a challenging brow. "Drop what, exactly?" He gave a pointed look around the house. "You're entitled to your grief, man. But we're not gonna let you wallow in it and drown. Take the trip. Think about something other than hockey for a bit. Maybe you'll have a clearer head when you come back."

He considered their offer. He wasn't exactly excited about going anywhere, but he recognized the kindness in the gesture. And maybe they were right. Maybe it would do him good to get out of town, away from everything that reminded him of his mom.

"Are you two coming with me?"

Colter grinned. "Only if you want us to."

Brooks dug up a faint semblance of his usual smile. "Now, why would I want to spend a week with your ugly mug?"

"That's what we thought." Grady pulled him in for a back-thumping hug. "I know everything about this is shitty. But you're gonna get through it."

Brooks gave in to the hug. "Thank you for caring. Both of you."

Colter pulled him in. "Anytime, brother. Have a good trip."

PREORDER your copy of *Summer Camp Secret* today!

OTHER BOOKS BY KAIT NOLAN

A complete and up-to-date list of all my books can be found at https://kaitnolan.com.

KILTED HEARTS
SMALL TOWN CONTEMPORARY SCOTTISH ROMANCE

- *Jilting The Kilt* (prequel)
- *Cowboy in a Kilt* (Raleigh and Kyla)
- *Grump in a Kilt* (Malcolm and Charlotte)
- *Playboy in a Kilt* (Connor and Sophie)
- *Protector in a Kilt* (Ewan and Isobel)
- *Single Dad in a Kilt* (Hamish and Afton)
- *Kilty Pleasures* (Jason and Skye)

SPECIAL OPS SCOTS
SMALL TOWN MILITARY SCOTTISH ROMANCE

- *One Fine Night* (prequel)
- *Before Highland Sunset* (Alex and Ciara) October 4th, 2024

BAD BOY BAKERS
SMALL TOWN MILITARY ROMANCE

- *Rescued By a Bad Boy* (Brax and Mia prequel)
- *Mixed Up With a Marine* (Brax and Mia)
- *Wrapped Up with a Ranger* (Holt and Cayla)
- *Stirred Up by a SEAL* (Jonah and Rachel)
- *Hung Up on the Hacker* (Cash and Hadley)
- *Caught Up with the Captain* (Grey and Rebecca)

RESCUE MY HEART SERIES
SMALL TOWN MILITARY ROMANCE

- *Someone Like You* (Ivy and Harrison)
- *What I Like About You* (Laurel and Sebastian)

- *Bad Case of Loving You* (Paisley and Ty prequel) Included in *Made For Loving You* (Paisley and Ty)

THE MISFIT INN SERIES
SMALL TOWN FAMILY ROMANCE

- *When You Got A Good Thing* (Kennedy and Xander)
- *Til There Was You* (Misty and Denver)
- *Those Sweet Words* (Pru and Flynn)
- *Stay A Little Longer* (Athena and Logan)
- *Bring It On Home* (Maggie and Porter)
- *Come Away with Me* (Moses and Zuri)

MEN OF THE MISFIT INN
SMALL TOWN SOUTHERN ROMANCE

- *Let It Be Me* (Emerson and Caleb)
- *Our Kind of Love* (Abbey and Kyle)
- *Don't You Wanna Stay* (Deanna and Wyatt)
- *Until We Meet Again* (Samantha and Griffin prequel)
- *Come A Little Closer* (Samantha and Griffin)

- *Just Wanted You To Know* (Livia and Declan)
- *A Love Like You* (Juliette and Mick)

WISHFUL ROMANCE SERIES
SMALL TOWN SOUTHERN ROMANCE

- *To Get Me To You* (Cam and Norah)
- *Know Me Well* (Liam and Riley)
- *Be Careful, It's My Heart* (Brody and Tyler)
- *The Matchmaker Maneuver* (Myles and Piper prequel)
- *Just For This Moment* (Myles and Piper)
- *Wish I Might* (Reed and Cecily)
- *Turn My World Around* (Tucker and Corinne)
- *Dance Me A Dream* (Jace and Tara)
- *See You Again* (Trey and Sandy)
- *The Christmas Fountain* (Chad and Mary Alice)
- *You Were Meant For Me* (Mitch and Tess)
- *A Lot Like Christmas* (Ryan and Hannah)
- *Dancing Away With My Heart* (Zach and Lexi)

WISHFUL MOMENTS SERIES
BITE-SIZED WISHFUL ROMANCE

- *Once Upon A Coffee* (Avery and Dillon)
- *Once Upon A Rescue* (Brooke and Hayden)
- *Who I Am with You* (Dinah and Robert)

WISHING FOR A HERO SERIES (A WISHFUL SPINOFF SERIES)
SMALL TOWN ROMANTIC SUSPENSE

- *Make You Feel My Love* (Judd and Autumn)
- *Watch Over Me* (Nash and Rowan)
- *Can't Take My Eyes Off You* (Ethan and Miranda)
- *Burn For You* (Sean and Delaney)

MEET CUTE ROMANCE
SMALL TOWN SHORT ROMANCE

- *Once Upon A Snow Day*
- *Once Upon A New Year's Eve*
- *Once Upon An Heirloom*

SUMMER FLING TRILOGY
CONTEMPORARY ROMANCE

ABOUT KAIT

Kait is a Mississippi native, who often swears like a sailor, calls everyone sugar, honey, or darlin', and can wield a bless your heart like a saber or a Snuggie, depending on requirements.

You can find more information on this *USA Today* best selling and RITA ® Award-winning author

and her books on her website http://kait
nolan.com.

Do you need more small town sass and spark?
Sign up for <u>her newsletter</u> to hear about new releases, book deals, and exclusive content!